Praise for
THE SUN WAS ELECTR

'I read this pure, pained, beautiful book in a single burst, and emerged from it with heart and nerves rinsed clean.'

HELEN GARNER

'This novel sifted like sand between my fingers, and then it pulled me under and made me weep, for everyone I have ever loved. I followed Rachel Morton's desire-line story wherever it took me, and I will always be where it ended up.'

LAURA McPHEE-BROWNE

'A work of shining, spare clarity that asks what it means to live a life of honest connection – to one's self, to love, to this world.'

PEGGY FREW

'Ruminations on belonging and the sense of being an outsider reveal how an insatiable desire for something more from life can sometimes cause harm rather than good. In a meditative and hypnotic style, Morton has drawn in-depth characters with complex relationships. The judges were impressed with how contained the story was and how the plot, while centred mostly on emotional stakes, remained unpredictable, but believable.'

JUDGES' COMMENTS,
VICTORIAN PREMIER'S LITERARY AWARDS

Rachel Morton is a writer living on Eastern Maar/Gunditjmara Country in south-west Victoria. Her poetry has appeared in *Meanjin Quarterly*, *The Moth Magazine* and various other publications. Rachel was shortlisted for the 2019 Australian Catholic University Prize for Poetry. *The Sun Was Electric Light* is her first novel and won the 2024 Victorian Premier's Literary Award for an Unpublished Manuscript.

THE SUN WAS ELECTRIC LIGHT

THE SUN WAS ELECTRIC LIGHT

RACHEL MORTON

First published 2025 by University of Queensland Press
PO Box 6042, St Lucia, Queensland 4067 Australia

University of Queensland Press (UQP) acknowledges the Traditional Owners and their custodianship of the lands on which UQP operates. We pay our respects to their Ancestors and their descendants, who continue cultural and spiritual connections to Country. We recognise their valuable contributions to Australian and global society.

uqp.com.au
reception@uqp.com.au

Cover design by Josh Durham (Design by Committee)
Cover artwork by Holly Anderson, *Bed*, 2024
Author photograph by The Wheeler Centre, TJ Garvie
Typeset in 12/17 pt Bembo Std by Post Pre-press Group, Brisbane
Printed in Australia by McPherson's Printing Group

University of Queensland Press is assisted by the Australian Government through Creative Australia, its principal arts investment and advisory body.

A catalogue record for this book is available from the National Library of Australia.

ISBN 978 0 7022 6889 2 (pbk)
ISBN 978 0 7022 7035 2 (epdf)
ISBN 978 0 7022 7036 9 (epub)

University of Queensland Press uses papers that are natural, renewable and recyclable products made from wood grown in well-managed forests and other controlled sources. The logging and manufacturing processes conform to the environmental regulations of the country of origin.

1

I MET CARMEN WHEN I wasn't well and had gone to the lake for the second time. The first time I went was ten years ago, when I still thought life would bring me things. Life had seemed to bring other people things, and I thought it might bring them to me. I didn't know it was too late for all that, even though I was still very young.

I met Dwain in the expat bars, and it was through Dwain that I met Carmen. Carmen had lived at the lake all her life. When I first met her, she seemed like a queen. She was haughty and she was arrogant and she had the most beautiful hair. Later on, I saw her differently, but that was how she seemed when we first met.

I went to the lake because my life in New York hadn't worked out, and my life before that hadn't worked either. On the outside I seemed to be functioning well, but inside I had the feeling that nothing had meaning and also that everything was fake. Even the waves of the sea looked fake. I knew the waves of the sea were real, but when I looked at them from the side of the boat on the way home from a camping trip, they looked fake, as though we were on a movie set and the sea was a giant swimming pool and the sun was electric light. Nothing seemed real, and to feel real, I imagined, was the fundamental thing, the thing you needed before anything else can begin. I thought if I was going to fix my life, I would need to get to where things felt real.

Things had not been good. They had never really been good, but for a long time I had believed that things would get better if I really tried, as though life was a fight that you could actually win. I found there was nothing left to try. I was sick of it. I was sick the way you feel when you have eaten too much and then arrive at a place where they offer you food, which you don't want but it would be rude to refuse.

I had moved to New York five years before. New York was the furthest place I could find from my hometown in north-east Victoria, not in distance, but in its largeness, which I thought might cover me. I moved there and I made a life and I did all the usual things. I went to work. I did the grocery shopping. I cleaned my apartment on Saturday mornings with the windows open to the street. I played the same CDs over and over again. On the outside, I lived a normal life. But, inside, life didn't make sense to me.

I started with the lists in the fifth year I was there. I did it as an exercise. I imagined I was dying, and I made lists of what I would do. I made lists for different periods of time, if I had just one day left, one month, or one year. I tried five years too, but that was diffuse and too far away to get anything good. Each morning before work I went to a diner and drank coffee and worked on my lists. I wrote throughout autumn in the wild rains when wet leaves stuck to the windowpanes. Winter came and I wrote and still I found nothing that I wanted to do. But the trying had given a rhythm to my days. I got up early and I dressed quickly now; I had somewhere to be.

Life seemed to be mainly about love, about love and staying alive. I did not love anyone back then, but I remembered that, once, I had loved a place. I remembered the lake, that it existed still, that I had been there, that I could go back again. I had loved the lake and I had not really loved anything since. That was part of how I wasn't well.

I had loved the lake. I could go back. Leaving was easy. Staying was harder, but I could deal with that later. That's what I was thinking when I decided to go back.

I gave notice on my apartment. I quit my job. I called a thrift store and they collected my furniture. I booked a flight for the end of the month. I lived on the floor, sleeping on a camping mat. Each day, I made trips to the thrift store to donate a bag of things. Finally, everything that I owned fit in a single bag.

In the last few weeks before I left, spring had started to arrive. I could feel my life ahead of me. I could smell the coolness of the lake as I walked the concrete streets. Around me there were people shouting and there were traffic jams and loud cars, and all I could hear was the sound of waves falling on the shore like a metronome.

And, like that, I went back. The thought crossed my mind that it might be a mistake. But it might also be right.

—

On the plane to Guatemala, I didn't sleep at all. The man sitting next to me ate nuts from a bag. He ate loudly and crunched the packet and looked for the crumbs at the bottom. The flight attendant offered us snacks from a basket resting on both of her arms. I couldn't eat. I couldn't read. I flipped the pages of my book where it sat on the tray table.

When the plane landed, some passengers clapped and some even kissed each other. It was early afternoon. I collected my bag and caught a taxi to the bus station. There were no lanes on the highway from the airport into town, and the edges of the road were made of loose gravel. Cars drove in their own haphazard lanes and moved around all over the place. At the bus station I waited inside while they threw my backpack on the roof and collected other passengers, then a younger man made a signal to me that it was time to leave, and then we left.

The bus trip was long and full of tight turns through tiny mountain towns. We passed brown farms with brown dirt and brick huts, and chickens that were cream and terracotta and brown. Tired woven clothing hung outside on lines of string tied between trees. Baskets of dusty vegetables sat on the steps outside the front doors.

Panajachel was a small lake town with one main street that ran from the top of the hill where the bus dropped me off all the way down to the lake. When we arrived, I walked straight to the lake. Along the road were hotels and stalls and during the day the local people sold woven clothes and beaded jewellery and various types of food. It was too late in the day for them now and they had all packed up. I could see their boxes wrapped in blue tarps, chained and padlocked to the wire fence. A young man in a long t-shirt walked close to me and then swerved away, swinging his arms out wide as he walked, calling out to no-one in particular.

I kept walking and I saw the lake, just the very top of it; it sparkled like jewellery in the afternoon heat. I reached the shore and took off my shoes and sat down. The sand was gritty, half sand and half dirt, laced with twigs and rocks and leaves. I rubbed my toes in it. Rubbish floated in the water near my feet, old rubbish, cloudy and pale with time. My back was sore and hot from the bus trip and from my backpack. A breeze reached the shore where I was, like a message. I felt relief. As though, by coming here, I had stretched out my life just a little bit, making it wider, the way you stretch out dough. I stood up to go and I felt tall and strong now under the hot sun. I had left and I had made it here and that made me feel strong. I put my backpack on.

The hotel I had booked two days ago was on a small lane off the main street. It had been painted long ago and now it was covered with dirty water stains. Paint cracked and peeled in the corners. But it was a cheerful hotel and it smelled of soap all the way through, through the entryway, over the tiled walkway that ran next to the internal patio, and inside the room itself, which was as small and sparse as a nunnery, with two single beds and a wooden desk in between with a high-backed wooden chair. There was a small wardrobe too, and this scared me and I didn't open it, and after a few days I turned it to face the wall. The window was high, too high to see out. It was open and, as I entered, the curtain lifted with the breeze, as though it was welcoming me.

After a few days at the lake my life became metered and contained. I looked for and found a swimming spot and I went there every day. Wherever I walked, I smelled corn and smoke. The streets were dusty beneath my feet.

I walked through the town and to the edge of town. I didn't go any further than that because people I spoke to told me not to. They told me I would get kidnapped, or maybe worse, if I went too far. Panajachel was not very big though and soon I had walked all over town, and I kept ending up at the lake. I sat there for hours at a time.

The days became a singular thing. I let myself sleep in. I walked to a stall in the street and bought tortillas and refried beans. I bought coffee too; it was weak and warm and it tasted of earth. Mornings at the lake sparkled with light; the sun warmed the jetty and the sand. When it rained, fat drops fell on the lake and they sank and disappeared. I didn't listen to the radio; I didn't read. Each night I slept for twelve hours at least. I slept the sleep of a worn-out child.

After a week at the lake, it started raining overnight and not just in the afternoons; the mornings were wet and heavy. I started going to the market. The market had once been outdoors, but now it was more indoors than out; each stall was covered with a makeshift roof and blue tarps hung on the sides as walls. It was dark and the floor was packed dirt. The aisles were narrow. At one stall they sold breakfast food and they had hot chocolate in huge pots. The first morning that I went to the market, I went there for breakfast. I sat at the counter, on a high stool. I had tortillas and eggs and cheese, and hot chocolate too. The woman brought it to me without saying a word and she walked back to the stove. She lifted the lid of another large pot; a cloud of steam came out. It smelled of warm corn. I didn't think of home.

2

THE FIRST TIME I SAW Carmen, she was walking down Calle Santander, which is the main street in Panajachel. She walked as if she had somewhere to be. Nobody walked like that in Panajachel. She walked like she was angry and the way she walked told you not to talk to her, even though you wanted to. Her hair was long and yellow and shone like gold right there in the middle of the street. Her clothes were strange; she wore a man's shirt and pants that were baggy and different shades of brown. Everyone noticed her on the street. Some people noticed her and didn't look, but everybody noticed her. When she walked past me, I felt a thrill. I could smell her shampoo, and incense too.

The second time I saw her was the night I went out to the bar. I had been at the lake for three weeks and I hadn't spoken to anyone, except the woman who cleaned my room every day and the woman who worked behind the front desk, who picked her nails and talked softly on her phone. I had gone to the café, El Nahual, a couple of times, and I could have spoken to other people there. But I didn't. I ate my meal and drank coffee and then I went back to my room. I noticed the other tourists who were eating on their own; I felt sad for them, but I didn't feel sad for myself. They were timid and seemed to want friends. I knew I didn't need anyone.

One day, I decided to sit downstairs in the internal patio of my hotel. I had taken down a book from the 'free books' bookshelf. It was a book called *Mexico* by James A Michener. I was reading at the table that was next to the garden bed, and at first I felt uncomfortable and conspicuous, then I felt that the patio was mine, then I forgot about the patio and about everything as I became absorbed in the book. It was a fictionalised account of the colonisation of Mexico. It felt real even though it was made up.

I heard but did not really notice when two people sat at the table next to me. They spread out their things and started sorting them as though the patio was their living room. The woman was thin and athletic, with long wet curly hair. The man was the same size as the woman and he wore his black hair short. They spoke Italian to each other and when I looked at them they stopped talking and smiled at me.

They were friendly. They pulled out some bread and some wine. They introduced themselves as Olivier and Sofia. They poured three cups and handed one to me, and then they handed me some bread and cheese. We ate together and they asked me about my life and I asked them about theirs. It was easier for them to talk about their lives and I asked them a lot of questions. They told me they were travelling, but they were tired of it. There had been no jobs at home and they had gone travelling instead of being unemployed, but they were tired of it now and they wanted to go home, even though they knew what that would mean for their lives. The wine had been enough for one cup each and when it was finished they decided they wanted to go to the bar.

They did not invite me specifically; they assumed I would go with them and they packed up their things and told me they would be back down in ten minutes, and we could all walk to the bar together.

I did not want to go out that night, and I did not want to go to the bar. This couple was nice but not interesting. But I was trying to do things differently to how I had done them before, so I went.

El Nahual was a café during the day and at night it became a bar. In the day it was light and open and bright, and people were polite and spoke quietly. At night it became a steamy place and there were no small groups, just one mass of people who were trying to forget, or improve, their lives.

At night it was a rowdy place. It was much busier than during the day. Some of the tables had been moved from the floor. Some people sat at tables along the wall, but mostly people stood around and held their drinks in their hands. I entered with the Italians and I was hit by a wall of sweat and noise and heat. There was a band playing in the corner and some people were watching it; most were not. Olivier went and got us all drinks. Sofia looked around and bobbed up and down to the music and she smiled at everything.

I watched the people and I had that feeling again that nothing here was real. Like the time with the waves. I felt separate, as though I was watching through a screen. There was nothing here for me.

I signalled in the noise to the Italians that I was going to the toilet. They were moving around so much that they were almost dancing now. The toilet was out the back, through another room. On my way through I saw the girl from the street, the one with the long blonde hair. She was sitting on a table, not on a chair, surrounded by a group of people who were standing. The people around the woman looked like Guatemalans from the city; they were shorter than her and had long black hair and wore rock t-shirts with the sleeves cut off. The Guatemalans from the lake did not dress like that; here, the women mainly wore Mayan clothes, the men wore collared shirts and baseball caps. This was her, the woman I had seen in the street.

In the street she'd been alone and wore the baggy brown clothes; she had seemed preoccupied. Now a light seemed to shine from her. Her hair was out and brushed long and it shone. She wore a floor-length blue kaftan. The kaftan was not the fashionable sort, it was not delicate like silk. It was a proper seventies heavy-cotton kaftan and it was unfashionable and it was strange. It did not drape elegantly but stuck out around her legs where she was sitting on the table. I knew she was strange. I wanted to know her.

The group of people around her were laughing and talking and slapping each other. The kaftan woman was not saying much. She watched them quietly, unselfconscious, like a teenager, or like she was far away. Then, suddenly, she changed; she raised her glass and said something and they all cheered. I would never be like her. She was the only real thing in the room.

When I passed her again on my way back out, she looked at me quickly, hard like a cat. She had cold green eyes like a cat too, and freckles on her nose and her face. I almost stopped, but I kept walking back into the other room. I felt her behind me but when I turned back, she was no longer looking at me but she was leaning on the shoulder of one of the guys, and they were laughing.

In the front room the Italians were drunk and now they were dancing properly and not just bouncing around. Everything felt fake again. It felt even more fake than it did before. I took my jacket from the chair and walked into the street without saying goodbye.

Outside, I was glad for the fresh air, and the coolness, the sudden solitude. The silence made things seem real again. Cold rose from the cobblestoned street. The hotel was not far and I walked slowly. The moon was bright. I had tried, I said to myself; I had tried and what I had tried had not worked. I would keep trying, I promised myself, right there in the street. But I would have to try something else.

3

The morning after the night at the bar, I felt old and somehow real. I realised that the lake would not solve my problems and that nothing would solve my problems. I gave up trying and giving up felt liberating, for about fifteen minutes at a time.

It was a Saturday, and the sun was warm. The breeze that came up from the lake was cool and because the lake breeze was cool, the sun's warmth felt beautiful on my back and the warmth reached into my bones. I had heard about a walk in San Marcos, which was two towns over, across the lake. I decided to try to find it.

I packed a bag and walked to the pier. The sun warmed the concrete of the narrow footpath and I could feel the heat through my sandals. I caught the boat and sat at the back; there were other tourists, but I didn't talk to them. From the boat, I saw a shady area full of reeds and then I saw a cliff. The sun shone. The wind made ripples on the water.

Lake Atitlán was huge and deep; the waves were small and rhythmic. When the wind blew, it blew ripples over the water, and when boats passed, they made choppy waves.

We arrived at the jetty and I put on my hat and I started to walk. I had the pleasant feeling of having somewhere to go and going there using my feet. In San Marcos, there were small dirt tracks and trampled weeds and feral dogs, and it was fine. It was midday and the sun was high and even hotter than before. I walked towards the general store to buy a bottle of water.

Outside the store, three older men sat on white plastic chairs; a bottle of aguardiente sat on a crate in the middle of them. They stopped talking when I came near and they stared at my back as I paid the shop woman. I wanted to drink the water right away but I decided to keep going. They started talking again as I walked away, louder now, talking towards my back. I kept walking until I couldn't hear them anymore.

I walked through the town up to where the town ended and the track started. The person who told me about the track had told me to look for the trees, two trees, they had said, that were on the edge of town. I couldn't miss them, they had said, one was black and one was white, they stood like poetry. I found the trees and I followed the track and it led around the lake and then wove up into the cliffs. At one point you could go either up or down. If you took the lower path, you ended up in the next town; the higher path took you to the top of the cliff. I took the higher path and kept on walking.

Somehow, though, I got lost, and instead of ending up on top of the cliff, the path petered out and ended halfway between the cliff and the village below. On both sides there were prickly bushes and they scratched me as I passed. The path narrowed.

This was definitely not the right way. Where the path ended there was a small clearing. I was sweating and swearing with the heat of the sun and the steepness and the slipperiness. I had almost fallen lots of times with all of the loose stones. I was not enjoying myself anymore and when I saw the clearing from the path, I said loudly 'Thank god' and then I heard someone laugh. I turned the corner and came out from the trees and there was a woman with short hair, just sitting there.

The woman was sitting on a rock and hanging one leg over the side. She was wide and strong and when I looked at her, I thought of wood, or of earth. She seemed good and calm and practical.

She began sorting through her backpack and half looking at a map she had unfolded on the rock in front of her. I glanced at her as I walked past to the patch of grass on the other side of the rock; I smiled quickly and then turned away. I opened my backpack and pretended to search for something while I tried to figure out what to do. I had thought I would rest. I couldn't rest now, with the woman with short hair just sitting there. I felt her watching me. I pulled my jumper out even though I was hot. I had a drink of water.

The woman spoke. 'It is very hot here today. Hotter than it has been all week.'

I swallowed the water and turned to her. The woman was looking straight at me. She sounded French.

'It really is,' I said. 'I had to buy this out on my walk.' I waved the empty bottle of water in the air and the drops shook from side to side.

'Oh, there are walks around here? I didn't know they exist.'

I was embarrassed. 'Well, there's supposed to be a walk. I was looking for a path to the top of the cliff. I didn't find it though.'

'It seems there is not much to do here. I was thinking of going and checking out the lake.'

I didn't say anything. There was silence now and I could smell the fresh smell of the short prickly trees that had scratched me.

'Have you been here long?' the French woman said.

'I'm just here for the day,' I said. 'But do you mean the lake? I've been in Panajachel for three weeks.'

She laughed. 'I don't know what I mean. The lake. Yes. Why not.' She laughed again and moved a hand through her hair and her hair stood up on one side.

'And you?' I said, still trying to look busy.

'The lake or this town?' She watched me and her eyes shone. She jumped off the rock. 'My name is Emilie.' She stuck out a hand.

'I'm Ruth.'

'Okay, Ruth. You've got ten minutes to rest. And then we're going down to the shore.'

We stopped at the general store on the way down and we bought two small bottles of beer. The shop was quiet; the tables where the men had sat were empty now. The air was getting cooler. The sun was low and it was almost touching the volcano on the other side of the lake. We opened the beers at the general store and then walked down to the water. We sat on the jetty with our feet hanging free.

Emilie told me that she was half Italian and half Swiss and she had grown up in Switzerland, in the French-speaking part. She laughed and said, 'Nothing but cows and alps and cobblestones.'

Her skin was olive and her body was strong, and she had a slowness to her that reminded me of mudbricks or maybe of homemade bread. Next to her I felt like sherbet, full of jesters and somersaults.

I learnt about Emilie's life. I learnt that she was the same age as me, that she was a sociologist for a French university, that she had come to Central America to work on a project doing field work in Mexico. She was travelling for a few weeks before she started her job. She had left Switzerland at eighteen and she had not gone back. She had lived in New York for a while too, and we worked out we had lived there at the same time.

Emilie talked about when she lived in New York. We'd had very different lives. Emilie, then, was surrounded by people, all the time, she said, and she rolled her eyes. She lived with her American girlfriend and she worked in a small team who went out together on Friday nights, first as a group to the whiskey bar and then, a smaller, drunken group, to a karaoke place. Emilie and I wouldn't have walked the same streets, we figured out; our neighbourhoods didn't overlap. It was like we had lived in two different cities in two completely different times.

Emilie showed me a photo from then. Her hair was longer, almost touching her shoulders. She was heavier too. In the photo Emilie had her arms stretched around the shoulders of the people sitting either side of her. They were in a restaurant. Her eyes were flat and her smile was wide.

She had lived there for two years. When she talked about New York, I could feel again the soft breeze and how surprising it was as it moved through the summer parks and came out fresh over the concrete footpaths as though it was the countryside and not city streets. I remembered the smell of coffee in the cafés and the nasal, angry shouts and the pinched look of the men. I had forgotten how lonely I was back then. I thought of Emilie, of the photo, of her eyes. Maybe we did know about the same thing.

We stayed at the lake until it started to get dark. Finally, the mosquitoes got so bad that we left. Emilie was staying in Panajachel too and we caught the last boat back.

We arranged to meet for breakfast the next day. We met at seven in the morning. Emilie didn't like to sleep in, she had told me yesterday. She was already at a table when I arrived at the café that looked over the lake. There was the fresh morning smell of sunlight on the cobblestones. Emilie had bare feet.

She raised her head when I got near. 'I ordered you a coffee,' she said. It sounded like an apology. We were the only ones there, it was so early. I felt glad to see her, really glad, the gladness stretched down to my toes. I looked at Emilie, at her short thick hair stuck up from sleep that she had wet and tried to flatten out. Now it was both wet and sticking up. I looked at her wide shoulders and her soft arms, at her flannel shirt and at the wideness of her, both inside and out. She sat on an angle that made her body seem like a triangle.

The waitress brought the coffee and we waited until she went away. We watched each other without using our eyes. There was a pleasant tension, like a surprise.

Emilie told me about her work. We drank coffee and waited for breakfast. At one moment, Emilie pressed on my bare foot with her own and smiled and raised an eyebrow. Now she was asking me about my life.

'But what will you do here? How long will you stay?'

'I don't know. I don't have any plans. I'll just see.'

'So, it's kind of like a holiday?'

'I suppose so. But it's also real life. You have to be able to take some time to think. You know? You shouldn't always have to be doing things. But holidays, no. No, I don't think so. On holidays you have somewhere to go back to.'

'And your family?'

I shook my head slowly and smiled, tired suddenly. I took a sip of coffee.

'But where are they? Are they in Australia?' Emilie asked.

'Yep. We're not that close.'

'And you have friends in New York?'

'Kind of. I sort of lost touch with them. I went through some stuff in the last few months I was there. I didn't see them much anymore, and anyway, I'm gone now.'

Emilie looked like she didn't understand.

I turned the conversation around. 'What about you? Like, family and stuff.'

Emilie shrugged. She shrugged a lot, I noticed. 'I have them. Well. Some. My mother is in Switzerland. My father died a few years ago. I have some friends in New York.'

'That's nice. Do you talk to them a lot?'

Emilie looked embarrassed. 'Not much anymore.'

'So, we're the same, you and me.' I said it firm.

Emilie blushed. 'I guess so. Well. At least in that sense.'

After breakfast we walked through the town just like I used to do on my own. Emilie watched and pointed at things. She asked me questions about the place that I didn't know the answers to. If things were reversed, if it was Emilie showing me around, she would have known the answers, I thought. Emilie was still asking me about what I was doing here. I couldn't answer her questions about that any more than I could answer her questions about this place. I felt lost, next to her, and I knew I was lost, but I didn't usually feel it like this.

'All I am saying is that you need one reason, just one, outside of yourself, to be in a place. Like string. You need to be tied to one thing at least. Otherwise you float away. Like the hippies here – poof! They are not tied to anything.' Emilie made a gesture of floating up to the sky.

'What's your string?' I asked.

'My string? My job.'

I felt tears come to my eyes, but they didn't come all the way out. But the sadness had made me quiet. Emilie looked at me carefully.

'Did I say something wrong?' she said softly, staring down at the ground.

'I'm tired today. Let's go down this way.' I pointed to a small street.

'Are you changing the subject?'

'I don't know what you want me to say.' I felt desperate and Emilie glanced at me and then nodded. She took my hand and didn't say anything. I was grateful, and relieved.

That night, I couldn't sleep. I rolled onto one side, then onto the other, and then I tried sleeping on my back. Emilie had gone back to her hotel and we had made plans to meet again the next day. I kept thinking of her and feeling strange things and then trying not to feel them. Emilie would leave soon, for her job. I was staying here. I had made a resolution to stay and to not leave for once in my life. I thought about this as I lay awake, listening to the cicadas.

Finally, I got up and put a jumper on and walked down to the lake. It was late, almost early now, almost a new day. The dogs were quiet and the whole town was still. The moonlight reflected on the shimmering water and the only sound I could hear was the water lapping in the dark. The boats bobbed up and down, knocking against each other. The lake breathed rhythmic, like a child asleep. I thought about Emilie. I didn't want this. It hadn't happened yet, but I could feel it happening; it was already much too close. I sat on the pier and waited until morning. I was energetic in an unhinged way.

Dawn broke and light came through and the air at the lake became cold. Mist hung over the middle of the lake. I walked up the hill back to my hotel. It was morning. I wouldn't sleep now.

4

Emilie had booked her hotel for four days, and after that she came to stay with me. She had planned on going to other places, but she decided to stay in Panajachel until it was time to go to her job. My room had a spare bed and at first we pretended that Emilie would sleep there. But Emilie slept in my bed from the first night and we used the other bed to hold our bags.

Emilie was the same no matter where she went. Here in Panajachel, walking into town from the pier, she looked around and commented on little things that she noticed. She was the same when she was with me or with a table of foreigners, or talking to the man who was driving the boat. She was the same anywhere, and she didn't seem to react to outside circumstances. I thought she would be the same even when she was alone. But at night she changed; she became pensive then, and serious, and a wildness burnt through her suntanned skin. During the day though, she was sure and soft and unflappable and this is how she was as we walked up the main street to my room in the hotel.

In my room, Emilie looked around and commented on things just as she had done in the street. She picked up the three rocks I took everywhere which were beside the bed and she touched them gently, thoughtful for a second, and a flicker of sorrow crossed her face. Then she turned to me and held up the rocks, and she grinned and said, 'What are these?'

I showed Emilie the places I loved in Panajachel over the next few days. I took her to the stall in the market where I had breakfast and I showed her my swimming spot, and we went swimming every day. Emilie took it in, watching and nodding and accepting this place as though it belonged to me and not to both of us, or to everyone. Emilie was interested in the world rather than herself or even the people she was with. The only exception was in bed at night when Emilie was interested in me alone, and she lay watching me and moving my hair off my face and asking me questions that didn't link up, like what did I think of the sky and did I remember the first time I went swimming alone, and had I ever cut the sole of my foot and what did it feel like. She seemed like a different person in these moments. I played a game where I put an expression on my face and asked Emilie what emotion it was. It was strange, but the emotion that Emilie guessed was almost always the opposite of what I meant. It was the first time I thought that maybe my face was not an accurate depiction of how I felt. Either that, or Emilie was bad at guessing it.

We lived together in my room as if there was no future and no past. Sometimes, over breakfast or as we walked to the lake, Emilie talked about her new job in Pátzcuaro. I listened with my body, trying to read her tone. Did she want to go? Did she want me to come? Did she want me to ask her to stay here with me? In the end, I decided that Emilie had accepted it and she wasn't thinking about the future in the way that I was. She would probably have agreed if I said I wanted to come with her to Mexico. She would have agreed as though I had suggested that we take the bus instead of walking to the market that day. Okay, she would say, neither happy nor sad, not even very surprised.

In the afternoons, we went swimming in the reeds where I used to swim by myself. The first afternoon that I took her there, Emilie came up behind me and wrapped her body into mine and we bobbed against each other in the water like seals. The rest of the lake stretched out beyond our hidden swimming spot, and I didn't care about it anymore, what lay beyond. From here I could see only part of the lake, and in front of us, far away in the distance, was a village with a white cross on the hill. I knew the town was called Jaibalito, but I didn't care about it. I didn't care about anything apart from where I was.

It was afternoon. We were lying on the bed, tired from the day. Emilie had swum far, and I had sat on the beach and read. It was hot and we had gone to a cantina for beers, and now we were tired, from the beer and the heat. I was reading an old paperback I had found that afternoon. Emilie was playing with her hair and she talked as though I wasn't there.

She told me about the time she visited Japan when she was young, in her early twenties. When she got there and visited the temples of Kyoto and all the little details were explained to her, the meaning behind everything, she experienced a feeling of completeness that she had not known before and had been trying to replicate ever since. She told me about her brother, who was one year older than her, who died when she was sixteen, in a car accident. He had been alone in the car and had driven into a tree, and he had told her things in the weeks before that he had not told anyone else, and Emilie knew that he had killed himself, or something close to it. Her parents thought it had been an accident though, and she never told them what she knew. When she was eighteen she left for Paris for university and she had been living overseas ever since. She didn't want to go back. She talked and she told me all this as though she were far away. Then, like someone waking up from a dream, she noticed me and she seemed surprised and she changed back into her normal face. She said she was hungry and we got up to shower and got dressed and went out to eat.

The night was soft and there was still some light left over from the day. I had showered quickly and now, outside, the breeze felt summery over my wet hair. Emilie grabbed my hand and held it tightly as if trying to say something without having to talk. When I glanced at her, she was staring at the ground instead of looking around and pointing at things.

We had dinner at the restaurant that overlooked the lake and, without meaning to, we had made the evening a special occasion. Emilie had ordered wine, which she didn't usually do, and I had some too. For the first time since we met, we had trouble finding things to say. A formal feeling had entered between us. We were awkward, suddenly. I didn't know if Emilie was waiting for me to say something, or if she was hoping I wouldn't say anything, or if she wanted to say something to me and couldn't, or something else entirely. I felt how young we both were. Before this I had always felt old. The last boat of the night pulled in to the pier and that was it, there were no more boats. Everyone was now in the place where they would sleep.

I tore up my serviette into little pieces under the table and dropped them into my lap. I felt sad in a misty and diffuse kind of way. Emilie was already gone, I felt. There was something heavy and unspoken between us. We walked home separately, a metre apart, and when we got home we went straight to sleep. Each one of us was on our own.

The following day it was cloudy and warm, but it did not rain. Emilie was polite with me, and we were being careful with each other. We didn't talk much. Other foreigners that we met asked us how long we had been together, and where we lived. Emilie was better at answering this than me. Whenever they asked, a part of me rose up, happy with the mistake they had made. When Emilie deflected them so well and so quickly, I felt offended, even though what she was saying was true, and also I didn't want to live with her as much as she didn't want to live with me. Believing in freedom was what defined me.

But now as we walked along the street under the sky that was full but did not rain, with Emilie holding my hand and nothing for us to say, I saw how simple and how nice it could be and I regretted that I always had to complicate things. I felt sad that my life had not been like this before. I didn't want freedom anymore. I wanted Emilie. I wanted a quiet and mundane life with her and I wanted to live in the world in which life takes place, not lost in my own inner fantasy.

I dreamt of a kitchen with a Laminex table under a fluorescent light. I dreamt of weeknights, of nights on the couch, of TV and falling asleep. I dreamt of sweeping the kitchen and Emilie texting saying she'll be home late and eating toast and walking around in bare feet on the cold floor. I did not want freedom anymore. The price for freedom was too high. Emilie and I were walking now and I had forgotten where we were walking to and I knew now that I would walk with her anywhere that she asked me to. I would not even ask why.

I didn't tell her any of this. But I felt her change. I felt her hand become firm in mine and her steps became steady and rhythmic. She was almost marching now; she had become strong; she did not seem hurt anymore. She was sure.

Suddenly she turned and kissed me, right in the middle of the street. Then she smiled and she took my hand and marched like she had been marching before.

I saw Carmen for the third time in the days before Emilie left. I did not know she was Carmen then, and I thought of her as the girl with the long blonde hair. Emilie and I were walking back from the market. Emilie carried the string market bag. We had bought salami and bread and cheese. Emilie had a craving, she had said, after all these tortillas and beans. We spent a quiet day sitting on the bed, eating our picnic feast. Emilie was on her phone;

I read. I was tired, and Emilie was far away. Our individual lives had entered that day. Some days it was like that; we remembered our lives. Other days our lives were easy to forget and we lived as though we would never part.

We spent the afternoon in the room and at dusk we went for a walk. It felt good to be almost invisible now as it was getting dark. It was a Monday and there was no-one in the street. A figure came marching forwards in the semi-dark and she made me feel slow and meandering. She walked fast, up the hill, towards us. She walked fast and, as she got near, I saw it was the woman with the long blonde hair. She seemed upset. She had almost walked straight past both of us when she noticed us and then she looked at me. There was the briefest moment of something, so brief that afterwards I was sure I had imagined it. She looked back down and passed us and kept on walking. I glanced at Emilie; she hadn't noticed her. Her head was down. She was thinking hard.

On the morning that Emilie left, I walked with her to the top of the hill from where the bus would leave. Emilie wore her heavy backpack and I held my wallet in my hand. We were both quiet, though from time to time Emilie tried to make conversation by commenting on things. But I could tell her heart wasn't in it and I didn't say anything. All I could hear was the swish of our feet.

Right before getting on the bus Emilie turned to me and looked me straight in the face. I hadn't noticed before that she was shorter than me.

‘Well,’ she said. ‘Time to go.’

I turned to the bus where the luggage was held.

‘I guess so.’ I looked out past where Emilie stood. I could see the lake.

‘Come here,’ Emilie said, and she pulled me in. She stepped back and she watched me. ‘You’re so strange,’ she said. She said it like it was a good thing.

I felt hot and rushed and I wanted to say something back but then the driver called us, snapping his fingers and gesturing towards the bus. Emilie squeezed my hand and let it drop as she walked away, and she climbed onto the bus. She disappeared for a moment and then reappeared, behind the glass, sitting high, in front of me. She waved and then looked through her bag and then at me. The bus started backing out and she waved again. Then the bus pulled away.

I watched the back of the bus as it moved slowly away and let out puffs of black smoke. It made jerky movements as though it would stop. But it didn’t stop and it drove all the way down and turned the corner and then it was gone. The people who had been at the bus stop dispersed and I gazed over the rooftops of the town. I walked away quickly as though I had somewhere to be. Pretending that I had somewhere to be, I found, made me feel less lonely.

I walked down to the lake and sat there for a long time. I had come to the lake for my own reasons, and my reasons were good and serious. I could not forget what I was trying to do. Emilie had been a new thing. But it was not real life, I told myself. The time with Emilie was only three weeks, a distinct block, separate from everything. I had to remember how lost I had been and not try to find shortcuts. I thought that if I let myself feel lost, and stayed where I was rather than trying to fix the lost feeling, maybe the lostness might grow into something else. But probably not for a long time.

5

THE MORNING AFTER EMILIE LEFT, I woke up and thought, *I have to make economies.* I realised that if I was going to stay, I would have to get a job. I needed something to do. I didn't want to be like those expats I saw who hung around in the cafés all day. Also, I was running out of money. I knew it would happen and I even knew when. I knew how much it cost to live here and how much I had. I started to make economies.

I stopped going out for meals and bought food at the market and prepared it at home. There were no more long afternoons at the foreigner cafés. No more trips to other parts of the lake every time I felt bored; no more stays in cheap hotels and meals out in tourist restaurants.

I stayed home, I went to the lake. I didn't look at the stalls anymore. The economies helped, and life was cheaper than before. But I still had the problem of my money running out. It was just running out more slowly now.

I tried to find a job, but I didn't know how to find a job in this place where I knew no-one. I didn't even know what kind of work I could do. The work I had been doing in the office in New York didn't exist here, and besides, I didn't want to do that anymore. I looked on noticeboards and asked the foreigners who lived here. I asked the woman at the hotel and the woman from the breakfast stand. They were vague and then they were relieved when I talked about something else.

I decided to move out of my room in the hotel. I found a house on the edge of town through a friend of the woman from the breakfast stand. The house was outside the main tourist area, on the top of the hill, near the river, in a quiet lane. It was small and it was out of the way, and much cheaper than the hotel. It had two square concrete rooms, a bedroom and a living room, and there was a tiny kitchen in one corner of the living room with a hotplate and a sink. The two rooms were surrounded by a garden on all sides that had been left overgrown. In the tropical heat, with all the sun and the rain, the garden was robust and firm. It felt fresh and wild and made the air around the house smell and taste clean. There were two white plastic chairs outside, one was missing part of its leg, and there was an unsteady white plastic table. From the garden you could see the sky and, because the house was on the edge of town and high, you could even see a part of the lake. You could hear it too, if the wind was right.

I moved to the house on a Saturday. The new house was furnished and all I needed to do was to pack my bag and leave. I walked to the house like I had walked into town on that very first day. The house had not been cleaned very well and that was the first thing I did. I was nervous and I kept busy; I did not want to think too much about what I had done by moving here.

I checked what the house had and what I needed. There were a few pots underneath the sink, there was a bed, a couch, and a desk and chair against the wall. I needed a kettle, and after cleaning for some hours I decided to go to the market to buy one. I felt nervous. I had committed to a life now.

I walked to the market quickly, I found a light aluminium kettle that looked like it was made for camping. By the time I got back to the house the day was almost over. I went to bed early, but I didn't sleep. Mostly, I lay awake, scared, listening for sounds I didn't want to hear. I fell asleep a few hours before dawn and when I woke, the sun was already high. I got up and walked around the house. The house seemed friendly now. The sun was warming the concrete walls and the house smelled clean and I liked it. I made coffee and sat in the garden and remembered my worries from last night and before, and they all seemed manageable now. This morning it really seemed as though I could make my life work.

Moving house and looking for a job kept me busy and gave me the feeling of future. Emilie had left, and afterwards I sometimes felt that I had missed a big thing, like life had offered me something that I should not have refused. The movement in Emilie's life made me feel stuck in my own. But I *was* stuck, that was the truth of my life, and I needed to find the way out on my own. It wouldn't have counted if I had found my way out through Emilie.

Since Emilie had left, I hadn't heard from her. We had not made any plans and we had made no promises. Still, she didn't text.

Neither did I. I pretended to be busy with my life, with the moving and the searching for a job and the economies and after a while the pretending became real and then a few weeks had gone by and Emilie was no longer in my life. After I moved house, I thought of Emilie in the past tense. It was as though moving had transported me to a different land, one where Emilie didn't exist. I didn't know why I thought like this, but when I thought of Emilie, I thought in past tense.

And I had to take care of myself. Emilie had her life, she had her job, her house, she even had colleagues, she had a whole structure around her. I was scrambling to find even one of those things. I was panicking. I had left it too late. I couldn't afford to think about love when I had to think about finding a job.

I was getting frantic. There was no work for foreigners here. I had visited the school, but they already had an American working for them and one foreigner was enough, they said, and she had been there eight years. I looked on the noticeboards in the cafés, but they were offering services to tourists, not jobs.

I had been in the new house for a few weeks now, and still I had not found work. I paced around the rooms and then I walked to the lake. The lake had become like a person to me. I squatted on the shore. The light was dim. On the weekends, city Guatemalans came to the lake to drink, but it was Tuesday today, and there was nobody here. The lake rolled in, the way it always did. No matter my mood, the lake was the same. It didn't see anything as a catastrophe.

I spoke to the lake, speaking quietly in case someone was near. I told the lake of the trouble I was having, trying to find a job. I told the lake that I needed work if I was going to stay, and I told the lake why it was important that I stayed. I told my story again and again. I repeated myself, I streamlined it until the story was just one line. Then, when it was dark, I walked back home. Nothing had happened. I made tea and went to sleep.

The next morning I decided to go out for coffee as a treat, despite my economies. The day was warm. I sat in the sun. I didn't feel panicked this morning although nothing in my life had changed. *Give it time*, I thought. *The panic will be back. Probably by this afternoon.* And I laughed out loud. That was how good I felt that morning. And then I saw Dwain.

I had met Dwain a few weeks ago, at the café El Nahual. Dwain had been born here and he had grown up here, but his parents were American. At first, he seemed like an American guy, one who had come here as a tourist and had stayed for too long. But he had not lived anywhere else. He wore a flannel shirt over a grey band t-shirt; he smelled of unwashed hair and weed. But there was a lightness to him, a purity, and I liked him as soon as I started talking to him.

His body was too big for him and he pretended a sort of extroversion, as though he was trying on someone else's suit. He was good in the way that people are good when they have suffered a lot without knowing it. He made an effort to talk to me when I went to the café.

He smiled a lot and he swayed when he stood, and when other people tried to make a joke, he laughed generously. He asked a lot of questions too, of everyone, and he listened to the answers, and then he nodded, not knowing what to say next. When anyone asked him questions about himself he became awkward and deflected in a joking way; if someone asked anything about Guatemala or about the lake, he pushed his hair back behind his ears and he became earnest and talked a lot. He was soft and easy to be around.

I had not seen Dwain for several weeks, but I had hoped I would see him again. That morning, I saw him walking towards me, walking slowly, as if he had nowhere to be. He might be able to help me. He had grown up here and he knew both the local people and the foreigners. I didn't talk to him then but seeing him made me remember him and I decided to go and find him later that night.

That afternoon it rained. I went to El Nahual earlier than I'd planned, while it was still light. The street was empty and quiet and wet, but El Nahual was full and noisy. The windows were fogged over with the hot breath of the people inside.

I stood in the doorway for a moment and looked around, and there, in the back, I saw Dwain. I went straight to him and stood among the group that he was standing with. They let me stand there, and Dwain noticed me and, like last time, he made an effort to talk to me. We talked for a while and then I asked him about work.

He pointed his finger at me happily. 'Carmen,' he said, 'lives here in Pana. She knows everyone. She will know for sure.' And then we forgot about it and didn't talk about it again until several hours later. We were still in the café and the woman walked in, the one I had seen in the street. I pointed her out and I said to Dwain that she seemed like a mermaid. Dwain turned to look and he smiled and waved at her.

'Carmen,' he called out. Carmen looked at him and then briefly at me and she walked towards us through the crowd. Dwain turned to me, suddenly serious. 'That's Carmen,' he said, and he looked at me.

'Okay,' I said, and I looked away.

Carmen hugged Dwain and sat down at our table. Her hair was soft and lay in little piles on the tabletop. For a while I listened while Carmen and Dwain talked. Carmen asked Dwain about people they both knew, looking at the menu and scanning the room. There was a lull and they were quiet and the Americans at the table next to us suddenly seemed very loud.

Dwain picked up some of Carmen's hair and playfully threw it back onto her, like throwing a rope onto a boat from the shore. He nodded his head towards me.

'This one needs a job. Can we help her out?'

Carmen looked at me in the same way that she looked at the whole room; she glanced at me, scanning briefly, but she didn't care. She leant back in her chair.

'I'm barely from here you know. Hey, you didn't come over for a swim the other day.' She punched Dwain on the arm and then laughed, then turned back to the room.

'Yeah, yeah, I told you only maybe. The guys wanted me to help them work.'

Carmen rolled her eyes. 'Whatever,' she said, and I laughed. Carmen looked at me and this time she really noticed me; she looked at me for a long time.

She held up her drink as though about to take a sip. ‘How long did you say you were staying here?’ Without listening to the answer but as though she was thinking about something far away she said, ‘You want a job? I have to go now. Come and see me sometime. I’m always at home.’ She took a serviette and wrote down her address. Then she leant over and kissed Dwain on the cheek. Her hair fell in his empty glass.

She looked down at me, serious. ‘See you soon,’ she said. She said it firm, like a command.

After she left I could smell a type of perfume that I had smelled before but I couldn’t remember where.

6

I WENT TO SEE CARMEN the very next day. She had her hair in a ponytail and she was wearing brown baggy pants and she looked pale and slightly unwell. After she had left last night, I asked Dwain all about her. He told me her parents came from California and they had come to the lake in the seventies and they had stayed here twenty years. Carmen was born here, like Dwain; like Dwain, she had grown up here. Neither of them had lived anywhere else; they seemed American, and they were in a way, but they had never lived there. Carmen still lived in the house where she grew up, and she lived there all alone. It was empty now; her parents had moved back and she didn't have any siblings. The house was on Calle Santander, right in the tourist part of town.

At her house, Carmen offered me boiled quinoa. We ate it plain, with olive oil and salt. Carmen seemed much younger today than she did at the café, or when I had seen her in the street.

She sat on the chair curled up in a ball and she hardly touched her plate of food. She watched me eat. She asked me questions about why I had come and what I was doing here and how my life had been before. I asked her about her life too and her answers were full of emptiness and were overly truthful in an embarrassing way. I asked her if she didn't get lonely here, in this big house, all alone.

Carmen looked straight at me and didn't blink. 'Yes,' she said. 'I do.' And she kept watching me, and I had to turn away.

She didn't talk about the job that day and I did not ask. On my way out, Carmen leant against the wooden doorframe that led to the street.

'Do you drink coffee? The coffee is generally terrible here.' She tossed her head and some of her hair caught the wind. 'The best place is down on the shore.' She looked at me now, almost shy. 'We should go there sometime.'

I said yes and stepped into the street. Carmen stood in the doorway and watched me leave.

We met like this a few more times that week, and I saw that despite Carmen's glamour and popularity, she was lonely and had decided I would be her friend. One day, she took me to the market. I had been here before, on my own and with Emilie, but it was different being here with Carmen. When I came on my own, I didn't go far and I stayed in the stalls around the edges. Carmen walked straight into the middle of the market and on to the very back. She walked quickly and I followed behind, half watching the market, half watching her.

The market had a dark and mysterious air and narrow passageways. There were stalls selling candles and feathers and meat, leather bags and wooden statues of Jesus and Mary. It was life in its totality. Incense wafted everywhere. There were chickens in cages and noise and dust and fruit and vegetable stalls. There was a small section for tourists; this was neat and smelled of the sawdust that was scattered on the floor.

I wanted to stop to look at the stalls, but Carmen was impatient and bored. She picked up blouses and dropped them down without really noticing them. I was electrified, but I didn't want to show it. I loved the incense, the embroidery, the low dark roof and the feeling of spirituality arising in everyday material things.

Carmen walked ahead, past the stalls, not even looking at them. I tried to keep up with her and touched things as I passed.

We turned a corner and at the end of the aisle was a small stand and a large woman.

'This is the place,' Carmen said, and she sat down on a high stool. She said something to the woman and they exchanged pleasantries, though neither one of them smiled. Carmen ordered for us and then leant her elbows on the bench as she turned to me.

I asked Carmen about her life again, the way I had done before. Her life still didn't make sense to me. She shrugged at my questions and she answered while she ate, talking through a mouthful of food. I asked her about her family. She spoke freely and with boredom. She told me emotional, personal things and mundane details with the same flat tone.

She told me about Dwain. His parents had come to the lake in the seventies and they had stayed for the whole of his childhood. They bought a house in Jaibalito and that was where Dwain grew up. When Dwain was seventeen, they moved back to the States and Dwain had stayed, but sometimes went to visit them. He even had some friends there, in San Diego where his parents now lived.

Carmen's parents had come a few years earlier than Dwain's, and the two families became friends. When Carmen was sixteen, both her parents got sick. They had taken bad acid together and it had driven them crazy, Carmen said. They had to go to the hospital in Guatemala City.

'I didn't drive,' she said. 'We didn't have a car. My parents couldn't afford it. So I had to call Dwain's parents and they were over in Jaibalito, and they had to drive here the long way around, rather than catch the boat. It took them over an hour to come. But they came and they took my parents away and they left me at the house. My parents never came back after that; after the hospital, they went back to the States and they stayed with my uncle and his wife.'

'What happened to your parents? Like, how did it work out?'

Carmen breathed out a long stream of air as though she was breathing out smoke. 'It didn't, I guess. My mom got better but my dad never did. They split up. My dad is in a psychiatric facility and my mum is a hippy in the desert somewhere. I don't really talk to her. I call my dad sometimes. He doesn't say very much.' She tossed her hair, and looked across the counter, and then around the market. 'It's funny, though, isn't it. The way they both went crazy at the same time. It's almost romantic,' she said, and she smiled at me, as though we were talking about the weather.

I felt a chill. 'That's intense, Carmen.'

'Probably,' she said, not looking at me.

We saw each other almost every day in those early weeks, except for the days when Carmen had to work. She worked at a coffee shop in the main part of town.

'It's for tourists, though. Don't ever go there. The coffee is awful and the prices are stupid. No, I'll show you where to go instead.'

'So why do you work there?'

'We all have to work, Ruth. There's no work around here. You take what you can get. The only good thing about it is I've been there so long now that I don't have to work weekends. They make the new kids do that. And it's casual. So I can take time off whenever I need. The management is shit. The pay is shit. But it's enough for me to live.'

One day, I went to visit her at work. I still didn't really know her yet and I sensed she could be tough but I didn't know to what extent. The café was made of dark-brown wood and white painted stucco walls. It had a hotel attached, and there was a gift shop too. I saw Carmen behind the bar, polishing glasses; she was wearing a white shirt and it was buttoned all the way up. She was sullen before she saw me; when she saw me she looked annoyed.

'What are you doing here?'

'I thought I'd come and visit you.'

'Ruth. I am at work.' She almost hissed.

Then an older Guatemalan man came to the bar and told Carmen she was needed out the back; he waited for her to go.

She threw the tea towel down and didn't say anything, but she looked at me and then walked out the back.

I didn't visit her after that, and we didn't talk about it.

One afternoon, Carmen took me to a cantina on the shore and we ordered beer. Carmen pulled her hair over the side of her head and looked out to the volcanoes and squinted in the light. She paused and scanned the room, then she turned to me.

'You want a job,' she said, like a statement. Without waiting for me to answer, she said, 'I might know someone. There's this family. Friends of my parents' friends. They are looking for someone to take take of their kids. Three boys, I think. Rich Guatemalans. You know the type. Poor little rich boys. Poor things. I'll give you their mother's number.'

She didn't give me the number though, and I didn't ask, and then the woman from the bar brought the beers to the table and set down a bowl of nuts. Carmen looked at me and smiled and punched me on the arm. 'Let's go for a swim after this,' she said, and then she laughed.

I laughed too, but I didn't know why.

The next day we met and we went swimming and then Carmen took me to the café that she liked that she said the tourists didn't know about. We sat, calm after the cold of the water and the warm afternoon sun. Carmen told me about the family. She told me that they were from the city and had a house in the city as well as here, but now the boys and the mother were mainly at the lake. The father was a politician and spent his time half and half, or even more in the city than here. She told me they lived behind the hill and pointed with her chin in that direction. She said that they were rich, that the mother was intense, the father was never home. 'I feel sorry for the boys,' she said almost quietly, pressing the crumbs on the table with the palm of her hand.

She thought the older boy was about eleven by now. When Carmen was younger she had babysat him. 'I can't be bothered with that shit anymore,' she told me. She looked at me. 'You might like it,' she said.

I told her that I didn't care and that I needed a job and that I actually liked children and it sounded kind of fun, as far as jobs went.

'Whatever,' she said, and she wrote down the mother's number on a scrap of paper she had torn from a magazine.

7

THE HOUSE OF THE FAMILY was behind a hill and surrounded by a tall fence. There was a security guard who was employed to be there whenever the family was home. The younger ones were aged five and three and they were called Rafael and Josue. There was another child, an older one; his name was Eduardo and he was shy. He didn't want to play, his mother had said, and I understood from the way she spoke, and the way she had looked after she spoke, that she was ashamed of him. I liked Eduardo the way I liked all shy people and I disliked the father for the same reason but in reverse. The father was loud and sat with his legs wide apart. He had a shiny red nose and slapped his older son on the back and either didn't notice or didn't care when Eduardo flinched and then tried to hide it.

The day I went to the house to meet the family, I guess it was a kind of interview, though when the mother opened the door she looked me over and started talking right away about the hours

I would do. The mother spoke to me about the hours, the days, the pay, and then she talked about other things. She talked as though she had no sense of what was appropriate and what was not. She told me that she wished she had girls. She said it straight and with an air of romance, the way one might say they wished they had curly hair. She told me how difficult the children were, then she turned and looked right at me and she said, 'But don't worry. You'll see.'

The whole time that she was talking to me she was tidying the kitchen. Behind her, through the window above the sink, I could see their garden; it was wide and open with manicured grass and lined on the edges with garden beds. There was an area close to the house with garden furniture like you would see in a home decor magazine; there were yellow-and-white striped lounge chairs and a low table in between. It looked like it was not used although it was kept very clean.

When I left that day I felt funny inside. I had a job, which meant I could stay at the lake, and I felt excited and most of all I was relieved. But there was something about the mother and the house and the boys that I didn't understand and didn't like. I ignored the thoughts and the funny feeling and I just went home.

Carmen called me that afternoon. She asked me how it went. I told her that I had the job and that I would start in two days. She was happy and for the first time since I met her, she stopped being cool and became like a young girl.

'That means you'll stay,' she said. 'That's so great. We can meet for coffee before you go to work. What did you think of them? What did you think of the boys? The mum?'

I told Carmen what I thought of them and she was quiet and I could sense her nodding on the phone. 'Yeah, I think you're right. Those poor boys. What the fuck are their parents thinking?'

I was shocked at her anger and how it didn't seem to match anything that I had said, but seemed to be its own separate thing that Carmen had been thinking about. I didn't know what to say back to her, but I didn't need to say anything because then Carmen told me she needed to go, and then she was gone.

On the first day that I went there to work, the mother gave me instructions and then left. When she left the house, she left behind a cloud of perfume, rich and strong and smelling of spice. The children didn't look at each other and they were silent for a few minutes. The two younger boys sat on the lounge room floor where they had been playing with plastic toys, and they sat there now, not playing anymore, glancing at each other and sometimes whispering. Eduardo sat at the heavy wooden dining table; he swung his legs and pretended to read comic books. I could feel him watching me without moving his head as I moved about the kitchen, looking around. I started making a lot of noise in the kitchen and I sang songs in Spanish and got them wrong. One by one the boys came in and corrected me and pretended to be exasperated with my errors, and laughed, throwing their heads so far back that I could see the outline of their teeth. Eduardo was the last to come in, he didn't act exaggerated but watched quietly and eventually smiled and his smile felt sweet like incense smoke.

Each day I arrived at the house at noon, even though the boys didn't get home from kinder and school until one. The mother came back just before six, still made up and smelling of restaurants. Sometimes the father came home on Friday nights; mostly he did not.

Whenever I could, I smiled at Eduardo, and in the beginning he ignored me. I played with the young ones as I was being paid to do. They were soft and cute and they adored me right away. The younger ones I grouped together in my mind as though they were twins, but they were not twins. Both had soft wispy baby hair and baby tummies and little legs. And they played together all the time; they did not leave each other's sides.

Eduardo was separate to all of this. While the younger ones were soft and full of laughter, Eduardo was moody and solitary. He sat alone and read or coloured in or did drawings in his drawing book. While the younger ones were round and healthy and stout, Eduardo was thin and delicate. It all made perfect sense.

And just like that, my new life began. I had a house, and a job, and I had two friends. I saw Carmen a lot and I saw Dwain on the weekends, always with Carmen though. Ever since Dwain introduced me to Carmen, Dwain and I didn't have our own relationship. But I loved him and he was gentle and he loved Carmen and he was good for her.

I didn't think about Emilie much anymore. It had been more than two months since she had left and she belonged to a different life now. Her world was inaccessible to me. I didn't think about her, but I felt her, all the time. I tried to imagine what she would say about different things as I went about my day. As I walked in the street, I looked around and I imagined what she would comment on. But I didn't know her well enough for that, and I was inventing her in my head. I didn't know if what was in my head matched what she was in real life.

I talked to her anyway. I noticed things and I imagined telling her about them. I imagined her pleased and laughing at me. Then I went to work, or I went to see Carmen and Dwain and we went to the bar or we walked around the town. I was too busy to be lonely now.

One day Carmen asked me about Emilie. We were at her house on Sunday afternoon. It was raining again. Dwain had been with us but he had caught the boat to go back to his house in Jaibalito. Carmen had put on an album and it was dark and she was braiding her hair. I was lying on the couch, on my back, looking up through the window at the sky.

'Whatever happened to that girl you were with?'

'Which girl?'

'You know. The one you were always with. The one with short hair. She kind of reminded me of a tree.'

'You mean Emilie? I didn't know you back then.'

'I could still see you when you walked in the street, Ruth. You weren't invisible.'

'But there are so many tourists who come and go.'

'Panajachel is small. I've lived here my whole life. I know everyone. I see everyone new.'

'Well. She was only here for a while. She was a tourist. She was never planning on living here. Not like me.'

'Where did she go?'

'Pátzcuaro.'

'Is that where she lives? She did look Mexican.'

'She's not. She's Swiss.'

'Oh. So she's working there?'

'Yep.'

'And will she come back?'

'No. Probably not. No, she won't come here.'

'Would you ever move there?'

'To Pátzcuaro? No. No way. I can't imagine it. I want to be here.' I paused. 'I haven't actually heard from her since she left.'

Carmen stopped braiding her hair and she crawled over and sat next to me. She put her head on my arm. 'Poor Ruth. We love that you are here. We don't want you to leave.'

I didn't know why she was saying that. 'Carmen, I'm not leaving here. I'm not going anywhere. It's a different life, the one she has.' I said all of that. But it didn't feel right.

8

It was a Saturday, and it was warm. I had been working with the boys for two weeks. I made coffee and sat on the step of my back door and stretched my feet out in the sun. I felt well. I felt something almost like hope. Life was bringing me things. Life had brought me Emilie. It had taken her away, but before that, it had brought her. I drank my coffee and felt the sun warm my feet. It moved further up my legs. She hadn't phoned yet. She said she would. But my life was here. Inside, the phone rang. It was Carmen. It was a beautiful day, she said. She had a few days off work. Did I want to come with her to Jaibalito to stay with Dwain in his house? I said yes.

Jaibalito was a village across the lake. From Panajachel, you could take a boat, and it only took ten minutes or so. The boats stopped at five and you had to catch one by then if you wanted to be home that night. It was Dwain who told me all this. He worked in Panajachel; all his friends were there, and sometimes he slept on their couches. He was working as a handyman for the foreigners, the ones who had holiday houses here. He mowed their lawns, trimmed trees, that sort of thing. He was shy when he talked about his work, but he seemed proud too.

On the boat to Jaibalito, Carmen's hair flowed behind her like a scarf. She seemed calm, soft like rising dough. She looked at me and smiled, and she closed her eyes. Next to Carmen, I felt dark and old, and stable in a way that I couldn't explain. Carmen shone so brightly, it didn't seem real.

Dwain was at the jetty when our boat arrived. He was wearing the same thing that he was wearing when I met him, the grey band t-shirt and an old flannel shirt. His hair was clean and smelled of shampoo; his face was clean and a little bit red. He put his hands in his pockets and he smiled at me, and they both started walking and I followed them. We walked along the edge of the lake until we came to a wide lawn, and then a white house.

There was a man in the garden with leathery skin wearing a broken straw hat. He nodded at us as we passed by to get to the house; he was serious. He saw me and his eyes lingered over my face. He seemed like an abandoned church. I walked quickly, not looking behind. I asked Dwain about him later, when we were out of sight. Dwain told me he was the gardener, and his name was Miguel.

'Why do you need a gardener when you're a handyman?'

Dwain laughed. 'Yeah. Well. I learn from him. Actually, he's the reason I got into it. He taught me, he showed me how to do things. He's been around since we were kids and he just sort of stayed. And now he helps me. A lot, actually. He teaches me things.'

Dwain took a key from a string around his neck and unlocked the gate outside the front door and we went into the house. It was cool and quiet inside. The walls were made of white stuccoed concrete and the floor was made of stone. Dwain said that no-one was home, he was the only one who lived there now. His parents had been back in the States for years and his brother was in El Salvador. He told me he always thought his parents would sell the house and that one day he would have to leave, but they hadn't sold it and this was where he lived. Carmen moved around the place with ease, as though it was her house, not Dwain's. She went into the kitchen and opened cupboards and pulled out a loaf of bread and a plate. She looked inside the fridge.

'Do you have any beans?' she called out without turning around.

'In the fridge, should be,' Dwain said. He was in the living room fiddling with the TV. It was like they were siblings. I stood awkwardly. I didn't know what to do. I walked around, trying to appear nonchalant. I picked up things and looked at them, pretending to be interested. The room was decorated with handicrafts. I was too old for this.

Carmen came into the living room with a plate of beans and bread and a pot of coffee too. She saw me moving around and laughed so hard that she leant forwards.

'Come on,' she said; she seemed like afternoon sun. She led me out the door.

'You coming?' she called over her shoulder, to Dwain. Dwain yelled something back, and we walked out to the lawn.

—

The garden was immaculate. Carmen licked beans off her thumb, then tossed her hair and lay down in the sun. After some time, Dwain joined us from inside, holding three beers in one hand. He gave one to each of us. He lay down on his side and flicked Carmen's head, then took some bread and dipped it in the beans. They talked about people they both knew, people like them, other American kids who had grown up on the lake. Some of them were addicted to cocaine, back in the States. Some had committed suicide. None had stayed, except Carmen and Dwain. Dwain was the only one who sometimes left and came back. Carmen rolled over and rested her head on Dwain's lap. It was not sexual, or anything, really. I tried to work out what it was. Dwain touched Carmen's head absentmindedly and Carmen looked over at me, then at Dwain.

'What do you think of my new friend?'

Dwain laughed, almost embarrassed but not quite. He glanced quickly at me and turned away.

'Very nice, Carmen. I knew her first, you know.' He spoke to me. 'How long have you been here now?'

'Almost three months.'

Dwain looked away and squinted his eyes, then nodded almost sadly.

Carmen kept talking. 'She's my new friend. You know where I took her the other day? El Olvido. She loved it.'

Dwain turned to me. 'Do you like it here? Do you think you'll stay? You have a job now, don't you?'

'I don't know. I mean, I was here years ago. And I was living in New York. Then all of a sudden I just had to leave. I left sort of all in one go.'

'Ah, you're one of those. The great escape,' he said in a movie trailer voice. 'We're familiar with it, aren't we, Carmen?'

'She's working for the Perillo family. She loves it here, don't you, Ruth? She wants to stay. I helped her out.'

'Good, good. That's good.' He talked like a tired old man.

Suddenly Carmen sat up and put her sunglasses on top of her head. 'I'm bored,' she said. 'Let's go for a swim.'

There was a swimming beach right in front of the house. The day had become hot. Carmen already had her swimsuit on underneath her clothes. I had brought mine and I changed at the house. Dwain went in the water in his t-shirt and shorts.

The water was cool and felt good after the hot day, after the lawn, after the beer. In the water I felt free again. I swum out away from the others until I was too far for them to speak to me. The sun burnt my face and stung my eyes. On three sides, there were volcanoes. I faced out, towards the lake and the villages that were dotted around. I turned back around to face the house. Carmen and Dwain were laughing and pushing each other under the water.

My gaze widened. I saw Dwain's house and I saw the rest of the village that I hadn't visited yet. Further up the mountain there was brown earth and scraggy bush. Up high, but not quite at the top, was a white cross. It was the cross I had seen that day with Emilie. I felt the dark water underneath me. I felt spooked. I swam back to Carmen and Dwain, and together we went back to the shore.

Carmen stayed at Dwain's that night. I had planned on staying there too, and I had brought my overnight bag. But after how I had felt at the lake, I decided to catch the last boat back to town.

I had a house there now. I wanted to be at home. And there was something about being with Carmen and Dwain that felt almost like a trap. Being around them for too long sometimes felt like being held under water. It was a mean thing to think. But it was true.

Emilie had been gone for a few months when I received a postcard from her. She had addressed it to the hotel I had been staying in before I moved to the house. One morning as I passed the hotel, the owner came out and stood in the street, wearing an apron and waving a card at me. She told me it had arrived a week ago and that she had been watching out for me.

The postcard seemed old, or old-fashioned at least. It was the sort of postcard that might have been sitting on a rack in a gift shop for twenty years. It was yellowed at the edges and the photograph was faded. I pictured it on a stand outside a store in Michoacán.

The postcard showed a picture of a coffeehouse in the mountains, surrounded by a plantation. There was a woman in the field with a basket on her back. I turned the card over and I scanned the words. I realised I was looking for the phrase *Wish you were here* and when I realised this, I felt ashamed. I studied Emilie's handwriting as if to find a clue, and I realised that I really didn't know her at all. Her handwriting was unfamiliar to me. She described her house, her street, her job and her daily routine. At the end she said, 'You would love it here,' and I thought about whether that phrase was different from *Wish you were here*, and how.

I started writing an email to Emilie in my head that very same morning. I was down by the lake, walking along the shore, thinking about what I would say to her. When I got back to the house, I typed up what I had said in my head, but I didn't send it. Then I went out into the garden and stood in the sun and I turned my face to the sky. I looked for clouds and for signs of rain, but there were none. I went inside and without thinking I pressed 'send'. Then I left the house to go to my job with the boys.

9

At the end of my first month with the boys, Carmen wanted to take me out to celebrate. Dwain thought it was a good idea. We went to the Italian restaurant on top of the hill; it had low archways and only the foreigners went there. For once, Carmen didn't roll her eyes. She was happy for me. She was making it special deliberately.

'We are celebrating her first month of work,' Carmen said to the waiter as he took us to the table. She was proud. The waiter didn't care. I didn't really care either.

We sat in the corner, near the fireplace. The top half of the walls were painted white, and there were brown bricks underneath. We ordered a bottle of wine and Carmen raised a glass and announced, 'To Ruth,' which Dwain repeated. The pizza came and it felt like we were children pretending to be grown-ups. Carmen sat up straight and ate the pizza with a knife and fork. Dwain drank a lot and asked me about my work.

'But what are they like?'

'Who – the family?'

'Yeah, the boys and stuff. The mother. Is the dad around?'

Carmen stopped eating and picked up her glass, and she held it in the air while she looked at me. 'Come on, Dwain. You know what they're like. A mother like that, a scheming, absent dad, how could they be any other way?'

Dwain nodded, quiet, then he took a sip of wine and turned to me. 'And what is it that you have to do? Do you look after them? Or are you there to teach?'

'I don't know. Both, in a way, I guess. I think the señora wants me to look after them, but in English.'

'The señora.' Carmen snorted.

'That's what Mariella calls her. I don't know her real name.'

'Well, let me tell you, it's not Señora, that's for sure. Who's Mariella?'

'The woman who cleans.'

Carmen put down her glass and pointed her finger at me. 'Listen to me, Ruth. You are not the maid.'

'I don't care. I don't care about that stuff.'

'Well. Maybe it's time you did. You're too soft. You're in Guatemala now. You can't let people walk all over you.'

'Who's walking all over her, babe?' Dwain said.

'Nobody, yet. But you know it too, Dwain. If she stays like that, it's only a matter of time.'

I didn't think that Carmen was right. She was right about me being soft. That I knew. Emilie would agree with that too. But I didn't think people would walk over me.

Carmen went to the bathroom and I asked Dwain about it.

He sighed. 'Ruth, Guatemala is a different place. You have to think differently here. Think about what this country has been through. Civil war for years. Then the gangs, and the war never ended, in a way. That sort of thing makes a person hard. And it happened to the whole country. The whole country is hard, in a way.' He picked up the bottle of wine and poured the rest of it into all three glasses. He poured it in Carmen's glass first, then in mine.

'So you think that Carmen is right? That people will walk all over me?'

'Carmen is from here. She has had a different life.' He paused and took a sip, and put his hand on the table, and seemed to think. 'You'll be fine, Ruth. And if you're not, you can leave. You're not from here.'

Carmen came back looking fresh and clean. 'What are you guys talking about?'

'You,' Dwain said. 'You and Ruth.'

'Of course you are,' and she laughed and sat down and pressed her head into Dwain's shoulder. Dwain looked at her like she was a small bird.

I had been at the lake for almost four months and I finally felt like a real person now. I liked my work taking care of the boys. I started work after lunch and I swam every morning, no matter the weather or how cold it was. It was a kind of discipline; I was training myself to do things separately from whether I wanted to or not. It felt good to slide into the smooth water, and to bob around in it, and it felt good to see the land from the lake; it made me feel differently about my life. And it felt good to come out of the water, wet and athletic and fresh, and feeling like a new person. When I got home and showered and my hair had dried, the old person was back, but it didn't matter as much anymore because I knew the new feeling would come again the next day, and that is why I went swimming every day, even when it rained.

With the boys it was different, as it should have been; with the boys it was clean because it wasn't about me. It was about them. What games they wanted to play, what snack they wanted to eat, and whether they wanted to be inside or out. With the boys it looked like play but it felt like work to switch off from myself and when I came home, I was very tired and I wanted to be on my own.

Sometimes Carmen came around, sometimes I wrote to Emilie, and sometimes I spent whole evenings on my own, drinking tea and staring into the night. Somehow my life had come together around me, almost in spite of myself. I felt relief.

One weekend, I went to Jaibalito. Carmen and Dwain were already there. The house seemed like a building site. Dwain was working on the house and Miguel was teaching him. There were planks of wood everywhere, and rubble, and piles of tools. Dwain stood next to Miguel and ran his hands through his hair and acted like a grown man. But he looked like a little boy and he followed Miguel around. He was getting stronger, though, and he had become tanned. Carmen seemed like a child or a cat, lazing about in the sun.

Carmen taught me to play card games, which I had never really done before. We drank beers in the afternoon and at five o'clock on the Saturday, Carmen made us cocktails. Dwain asked about Emilie; I gave a vague response and Carmen watched me with an amused expression, then had a sip and looked away.

On Sunday, I went walking by myself. I had never really explored Jaibalito before. I usually just went straight to Dwain's. You couldn't access Jaibalito from the road and the only way to get there was by boat. I thought that made it a special place. The town was plain and very quiet; there were huts, but no-one was around. I wondered where everybody was. The streets were brown. I heard some music and I followed the noise; it was an evangelical church with an amplified band. The village was tiny and I reached the edge, and then I went back to the house. Dwain had finished work for the day and he and Carmen were lying on the grass.

'Find anything interesting?' Carmen said.

'Not much.'

'Thought so,' she said. 'Here. Have a drink.'

Out of the blue, Emilie called me one night. She had been gone for months now and we had not spoken at all. We didn't talk on the telephone. We didn't send each other messages. There was the postcard, and there were the emails. Since I sent that email the morning of the postcard, we had been emailing back and forth. Then she called me and I remembered her voice and from her voice I remembered the rest of her. When she talked, it sounded like she was saying only half of what she had thought she might say when she decided to call. The rest she left unsaid.

I was happy she called. I had not called her. I supposed we needed time to get on with our lives. And I felt shy in the aftermath of our intensity. Like being hungover, when you wake up the next day and remember things from the night before.

I wondered if Emilie felt the same way. But she called me, and she spoke normally. I tried to talk normally too. I mainly talked about the boys and I listened to Emilie talk about her work. More than anything, we both talked a lot about the places we were in. Emilie really loved Pátzcuaro. I was in love with Panajachel.

After that first phone call, Emilie stayed in touch in a way I did not anticipate. I had thought of Emilie as independent and free and now she was calling me with regularity. She sent me photos every few days, beautiful photos of the places she visited for work, villages up in the hills. She called me several times a week, at odd hours each time. Each time she called, I felt she had something to say; each time she spoke about her life over there and she asked me about mine. She trailed off in the middle of sentences. When we hung up, I felt as though I had eaten a bag of popcorn instead of a meal.

Emilie talked about her job, how much she loved it, and her work; she spoke of the small house that she had found, and how much she loved it. Once, she told me how she felt only half alive ever since her brother had died and that it was good for her to be around so much life. Life, she spoke about life and how much life there was there, but how with that much life you get just as much death, and maybe she hadn't quite thought it all through. After one of her speeches like this, she stopped; I could hear her look up, and she made a comment on something she saw in the street.

I had been surprised when Emilie first started calling me, but it didn't take long to get used to it so that on the nights that she didn't call, I was disappointed and even a bit hurt. I tried to talk myself out of feeling that way; if it was warm, I went to the lake for a swim, or I played cards and listened to Bach, or I had a shower until my skin was red and my fingertips pruned.

Emilie told me things I would never forget. One day she called and said her mother was sick.

'Sick how?'

'Sick in the head. She's forgetting things. She gets things confused when I talk to her. I have no idea how she really is. She doesn't really have any friends left there. And, of course, no family. I might have to go back and check on her. I really don't want to. Are you there, Ruth?'

'I'm here. I was listening.'

'What do you think?'

'What, about your mum?'

'About going back to see her.'

'Well. I guess you should. Either you go back and check on her or you worry about it day and night.'

'Yeah. You're probably right.' She paused. 'Damn it. Well. I'll hold off a bit longer. I can't go now anyway. We're doing field work next week. I'll wait until after that and see. I could just go back for a week. It doesn't have to be a very long visit.'

'No.'

'No. You're right. Yeah. I'll go for a week. No more.'

Emilie and I spoke often now, and often we just sort of hung out on the phone. Emilie sometimes lay in bed, looking through her books, reading out passages she thought were interesting. I listened while I cooked. I brought the phone outside while I sat in the garden and ate. Sometimes we had a glass of wine and pretended we were in a bar. I felt confused; sometimes I felt a sisterly love for her. Other times, it was desire. When her name appeared on my phone, I felt a tingling. Each night we were a bit awkward at first. By the time we hung up, there was tenderness. It happened that way every single time.

We mainly spoke during the week, and on weekends I went to Jaibalito. I went there now almost every weekend. I didn't need to be in Panajachel. There were the bars and tourists, and I was bored of both. Carmen and Dwain were all I needed, and Emilie during the week.

I didn't talk to Carmen about Emilie, and I didn't talk to Emilie about Carmen and Dwain. And there were the boys. They were all separate now. They were all in my life but they didn't fit together and I moved from one to the next like a boat on the lake, moving between different villages.

10

I HAD BEEN WORKING WITH the family for a few months when the mother started handing me lists. Once, after she had come home from one of her afternoons out, she looked around the house and she glanced at the boys and she sniffed.

'There is a smell. What is that smell?' I didn't know what the smell was and I could not smell anything, other than the mother's perfume and the beans cooking on the stove and the clean, warm smell of steam rising from the pots. She turned to me and spoke to me like I was a child.

'Ruth, please. I like the house to be neat and tidy.'

I did not understand what she meant by that but from that moment on, I understood that she was unhappy with me. The next day when I arrived at the house the mother had already left.

Mariella pointed towards the bench. 'The señora left a note for you.'

I picked up the note and read it. The note was a list of household jobs that she wanted me to do.

The list said to wash the boys' clothes and put them in the dryer, fold them and put them away. It said to tidy up the boys' rooms and the floor of the living room where all their toys were spread out. It said to check their lunchboxes when they got home and to wash them, ready for Mariella to fill them the next morning. It said to sweep the patio and to arrange the boys' outdoor toys. I stared at the list and I wondered how I would manage to spend any time with the boys at all. I felt a panic rise. And then I got to work. I had one hour before the boys came home. I would do it all.

I worked hard and had mostly finished the jobs on the list by the time the boys got home. I still had to take their clothes out of the dryer and fold them and put them away; I gave the boys a pile of books to read while I worked and I set them up in the living room, talking as though it was fun. Eduardo sat at the kitchen table colouring pictures in his colouring book. The mother came home and looked around and looked at the boys sitting quietly on the floor of the living room, reading books and drawing pictures; she sniffed and said thank you, though she seemed unimpressed.

Each day from then on went like this, with the mother leaving me long lists of work. The lists became longer and I was no longer able to get it all done before the boys got home.

I came home tired every day now. It had been several weeks with the lists and the lists were getting longer. It became harder to spend any time with the boys. I was getting everything done but that was all I did. I no longer played with the boys or spent time with them, and they were sad and often sick. I was tired. I had had enough. I loved the boys, but I was being pushed out. It was an impossible task, what the mother was asking of me.

I walked home slowly after work one night. There was already a single star in the sky even though the sky was still light. I felt cold. I longed for a bath. When I got home there was a handwritten note on my door from Carmen; I pulled it down and put it on the table and I didn't think of calling her. She had sent me a message a few days ago and I had been too tired to reply. I sat for a long time, trying to decide what to do. Should I quit? Carmen would tell me to quit. Emilie would say I should get something more meaningful. Neither of those things felt right, and what I was doing didn't feel right either. Each day was a fight and I was losing it. Even the boys were becoming miserable.

I sat outside for a long time and didn't notice when the day became night. It was dark now and I had no solution. I could hear the neighbour washing her hair outside, I could smell her soapy shampoo. I heard her singing quietly. I heard her husband come home and they started arguing. I went inside and I went to bed. I didn't know what to do.

One night on the phone, I told Emilie about the lists of jobs the mother was giving to me. I didn't talk about it with Carmen and Dwain; I already knew what Carmen would say and Dwain would agree but in a kinder way. I wondered what Emilie would say. Emilie was grounded in the world in a way that none of the rest of us were.

'What kind of lists?' Emilie asked, carefully.

'Lists of jobs. Like, chores to do. But I don't get it. I'm supposed to be looking after the boys.'

'So that's the issue?'

'Yes, I can't get it all done. If I do all the jobs, I neglect the boys. If I spend time with the boys, I don't do the chores. It's like a catch-22. It's like she has planned it like that, to drive me crazy.'

'Ruth, that's so dramatic. Why don't you just talk to her and sort it out?'

I saw then that the world Emilie lived in was a different one to mine. She honestly believed that the problem could be solved by talking about it with the mother. That would probably even work for her. That kind of thing didn't work for me. I had tried that kind of thing before. It didn't work.

The next time I saw Carmen, I told her about the lists. I wasn't planning on telling her, but the words just came out. She reacted the way I expected her to.

'Why don't you tell her to go fuck herself. Tell her to do her own fucking jobs if she doesn't want to look after her kids.'

Dwain was also no surprise.

'Carmen, you know she can't do that. She'd get fired.'

They were like two different sides of the exact same coin. At times like these I couldn't imagine either one of them existing without the other. They balanced each other out like couples that have been together for years, who have one-half of a personality and rely on the other person for the other half. They had not learnt to balance themselves out on their own.

'What do you think she should do then, Dwain?'

'I don't know. The mother sounds crazy. What can you do with someone like that? She wouldn't listen.'

Carmen turned to me. She was softer now. 'Yeah, Ruth, she's crazy. You're going to have to be careful there.'

They were as little help as Emilie had been, though in exactly the opposite way. I decided to do it in my own way, which was to do nothing and just wait and see.

One Thursday afternoon, I finished work and walked home and when I got there, Carmen was there, waiting for me on my steps.

'You don't believe in messaging?' I said.

'*I* do. You never message back.'

But I was glad to see her. She looked happy today. I unlocked the door and we went inside.

Carmen sniffed the air. 'It smells like sardines.'

'It does not. Rack off.'

'Rack off? Rack off?' She threw her head back and laughed. 'Oh my god, Ruth, you crack me up. You really are a sixty-year-old man.' But she came up beside me and gave me a hug and I knew that she cared and was just having fun.

I was glad she was here. It had been a hard day. Another bad day with the family. I was tired. I felt itchy underneath my skin. I didn't want to talk about it, though.

'Do you want a beer?' I called out.

Carmen was in the garden, poking around. She called back, 'Do you have any wine?'

I had half a bottle of red wine on the bench and we sat outside on the concrete steps.

The garden smelled like wet earth, dark and cool. It had been raining a lot recently.

'How's work?' Carmen asked brightly, looking up at the sky.

'Don't ask.'

Now she turned to me. 'I thought that's what normal people talked about.'

'Are you trying to be normal, Carmen?'

'I thought I should at least try.'

I sighed. I looked out over the neighbour's tin roof. Beyond it there was nothing but sky. I felt serious.

'Don't. You're a million times better than everyone else.'

But I had changed the tone. Carmen had been playing around; I was being sincere. The words felt heavy when they came out, like a massage, they were so true. Carmen shifted from side to side. She had a strange expression on her face. She tried to laugh and it didn't come out right. She didn't look at me.

I understood. I had been too honest. I had meant what I said and Carmen knew it and she didn't know what to do. She couldn't make one of her quippy remarks, and she couldn't say 'thank you' and leave it at that.

I picked up a stick and dug into the ground. The dirt was soft and wet. A clump of grass came up.

'Is there any more wine?'

I pointed to her glass with the stick. 'That's the last of it.'

'Do you want to go out?'

'You know what? I actually do,' I said.

'Yay,' Carmen said, and she was back to normal again.

—

On the way out, Carmen messaged Dwain. He was already in Panajachel with some of his other friends. He would come and meet us, he said.

'Honestly, I don't know why he bothers with them. He's got us,' Carmen said. And she meant it and she wasn't joking around.

In El Nahual we stood in one corner and Carmen seemed shy. It was like she had forgotten how to interact. People came up to her, people she knew, and she was so quiet that I had to fill in for her. I wondered what was going on for her.

Dwain arrived and Carmen lit up and she hugged him happily. She put one arm around each of us and she said, 'Now we're all together again.'

We didn't talk very much, the three of us. The bar was filled with tourists who didn't have to work the next day. Neither did Carmen or Dwain. I had to work but I didn't care. It was loud. Occasionally one of us said something and we had to yell it twice, once into each person's ear. Carmen was bobbing and looking around. Dwain did some funny, slinky dance moves and made us both laugh. I had never seen Carmen happier.

We stood like that and watched the room and people came and some talked to us. After a while, Dwain bought us more drinks. I was dizzy now and the neon lights had become a rainbow string in the air. I saw two of Dwain. Carmen grabbed my hand and pulled me to the dance floor and I reached out and grabbed Dwain. We pushed our way to the middle of the area in the corner where people danced. Carmen closed her eyes and put her arms up high. Dwain bent his head and swayed from side to side in a move that looked cool and not drunk. I loved them so much right then. I hugged each one and then did my own dance moves and it felt good to be free of myself. The dance floor was sweaty and dirty and dark and right now this place felt better than everything else.

Carmen stepped in towards me. She danced close to me with her arms in the air. Dwain was behind her, lost in his world, dancing alone and not looking up. Carmen was really close to me now and I could smell her hair and her sweat. I was scared. I didn't know what she wanted. I was afraid that she thought because I had been with Emilie I might want to be with her too. I didn't think I wanted that. I loved her. But I didn't want that. I pulled away and I kept dancing, but further away, and Carmen stopped dancing close to me.

Somehow I got home and I fell asleep in my clothes. I drank a lot of water before I went to bed and I kept getting up to go to the bathroom throughout the night. I woke up early and I drank some more water and fell back asleep and then when I woke up again it was time to go to work.

11

After the night at the bar, it rained for three days. The rain was heavy and it did not stop, not overnight nor in the mornings. The roads were closed because of flooding and the boats stopped crossing the lake. The schools closed and because the schools were closed the people did not go to work. Everyone stayed home. You couldn't see more than two steps in front of you; the rain was thick and the sky was low. I didn't leave my concrete house. When my fresh food ran out, I ate oats and powdered milk. I wrote letters to people from my past, but I didn't send them.

When the rain stopped, my life had changed in small and simple ways. I went to work in the afternoons and I did whatever the mother asked me to do. Whatever she asked me, I said yes, as though saying yes was a kind of credo. I no longer got upset. This was my life now. I was too tired to fight. I was unfulfilled, and I was no longer asking to be fulfilled; in my misery I found a freedom that was new.

I involved the boys in the jobs. The boys joined in and they loved it because now I was light and more fun than before. It no longer mattered what the mother wrote on the list; each day the boys and I looked at the list with excitement, a kind of activity program for the day. I let the boys choose the jobs they wanted to do and I didn't care about finishing them. We were still working when the mother came home. One time she stood in the doorway and watched us fold laundry and Rafael put a pair of underpants on his head and collapsed in a fit of giggles. She folded her arms and sniffed and asked to talk to me outside.

'I do not pay you to make my boys work,' she told me in the hallway, loud enough that the boys could hear.

I was ready for this. I was strong. I felt my feet on the ground. 'You pay me to take care of your boys, not clean your house. You want me to focus on the boys?' I paused. The mother went to speak, then stopped. I continued. 'Then stop leaving me lists of work. If you want me to do the chores, don't expect me to play with the boys. You choose.' I stayed watching her for a long time after that and waited for her to say something. When she said nothing, I walked back into the room, to the laundry, and the boys.

For the next few days, I arrived at the house and the blinds were drawn. The mother opened the door and walked off without saying a word. The boys and I spent the whole day in the garden.

Sometimes the mother appeared in the window, holding a glass in her hand. I pretended not to see and when I looked back a moment later, she was gone again. Mariella moved about, serious. We stayed outside in the garden until the sun got low and it became cold and the mosquitoes came out, and then we packed up the blanket and the toys and we went inside. Each night I left everything in a basket by the door and the next day we picked it up and walked back outside.

I didn't see much of the mother anymore. She had stopped answering the door at all now and it was Mariella who let me in. One day, Mariella handed me a key and told me it was from the señora.

The mother still left lists, but there was not much on them now; they were written in a strange and wobbly handwriting. She left my pay in an envelope on the bench instead of counting it and handing it to me. Mariella whispered as though the mother was sick or asleep. The children held on to me more tightly now; they climbed on my back when I sat on the floor. Each day we moved further out into the garden and by the time we reached the fence from where we could see the lake I realised I hadn't seen the mother in weeks.

One day I arrived and took the basket from the floor and Eduardo walked up to me and pulled on my arm. He told me that his mother said we had to go to the lake. I knew that he was making it up, but I wondered now about taking them out. There had been an unspoken rule that I was not to leave the house with the boys. But that was before, and things had changed.

Before I left that day, I wrote a note asking the mother about the lake and I left it on the bench. The next time I arrived and let myself in, there was my note on the bench and underneath, it said 'Yes.'

The day was muggy but not wet. The boys still wore gumboots though. *Just in case*, they said, all serious. The younger ones held my hands, one on each side. In the street, I saw how the boys' clothes were formal and old fashioned. Their hair was combed to one side; they wore clean white shirts and pressed overalls. They seemed as though they were in the wrong time, or maybe in the wrong place.

The boys stepped tentatively down the cobbled street. The women from the stands smiled at them and the boys turned away. They looked at the fire of the tortilla stand and they coughed when they walked through the smoke. There was a man sitting on a step outside a shop, he had a small radio next to him. It was playing marimba dance tunes. The boys stared hard, at the radio and the man; the man jiggled his shoulders and smiled at them. They watched the lanky foreigners walking up the street. They held my hands tightly, one boy on each side; Eduardo walked behind me. We stepped forwards rhythmically. We reached the end, where the road curved, and then we were at the lake.

The lake spread out with generosity. We found a place on the beach and the boys took off their boots and stepped into the water. There were pebbles on the bed of the lake and their small feet curled around each stone. The boys stepped slowly and seriously at first, concentrating hard on what they were doing. The water was cold. The boys asked why. I told them it was because the lake was so deep. Josue looked out to the middle of the lake with his eyes wide and said he thought he might just stay here. There might be monsters in the water, he said to himself, as he turned over a pebble with his big toe. He stood on one leg like a ballerina, or an acrobat. He looked at me and smiled and then he looked back at his feet.

After that first day, we started going down to the lake every day, even when it rained, if it was only raining a little bit. If it was raining a lot, we walked around the market and drank hot chocolate sitting on the high stools. It was unbearable to be in the house; the energy there was heavy and stifling.

Sometimes, I heard the mother breathe or I heard the sound of her gold rings knocking against the glass that she always held now. Whenever I saw her, she was drinking whiskey and she didn't even try to hide it. Her suffering was the kind that destroyed you if you got too close. I was worried for the boys. There was nothing I could do. But still I was worried for them. I knew I was a fill-in. But it was good, what we were doing, going to the lake every day. The boys were getting stronger and more confident. The sun had made their small bodies brown.

One weekend, I went to Jaibalito. It was becoming spring and the sun was hot after a period of cold. Carmen was lying on her back on the lawn, with her sunglasses on, shading her face with her arm.

'You know, Ruth, when I was younger, I hardly smoked.'

Dwain looked over from the other side of the garden. 'It's true. You were so good.' He was watering the lawn. The water ran off the hose in a rainbow of beaded droplets, and the sun caught the droplets in its light before the water fell to the ground. It smelled cool.

'I was so good. I was smart too. Remember, Dwain, how the other kids would give me their homework to do?'

'You loved doing it too. I remember you at my house. I wanted to play and you shooed me away. You were so serious.'

'I wanted to get As for every single one. I had to find a different way for each one of them. It was like solving a puzzle.'

'Why were you doing homework at Dwain's?'

'I was at Dwain's all the time back then. I almost lived with them. My parents didn't mind.'

'Didn't notice, more like.' Dwain squirted the hose near us and then pointed it back at the garden.

'Like yours were so much better. They didn't even know we were there.'

Carmen spoke about how, before her parents got sick, she had already started coming to Dwain's. She came here on the weekends and lived with Dwain's family, *pretending to be one of them*. That was what she said. Then she lived full-time with them, for a year, after her parents left. She lived there while she finished school, though she still had the house in Panajachel. A year later, Dwain's parents left too, *to get real jobs and to be normal people again*. That was how Dwain put it. They went back and got jobs and they cut their hair. Dwain stayed. He was eighteen. He didn't want to leave and his parents believed in freedom above everything else, he said. So they left, and Dwain stayed behind in the house, and he was still here.

I asked Dwain about this.

'How did your parents afford a house here?'

'My dad's aunt died. She was childless. She left her money to my dad and my aunt. It wasn't a lot, but it was enough to buy something here,' Dwain said.

'They were lucky,' I said.

Dwain kept watering. 'Yes, they were. For sure.' And he looked briefly at Carmen, who was playing with her hair.

'Do you ever feel like imposters?' I asked, without knowing why.

Dwain looked at Carmen.

Carmen sat up and lifted her sunglasses to the top of her head. 'Why would you say something like that?' She was hard; she stared at me; she was ready to fight.

'I don't know. I mean, this isn't your land. But your parents could afford it when the locals couldn't.'

'Whose land is it?'

'I just mean, you're not Guatemalan. You're not from here.'

Carmen took a breath, and she spoke very slowly. 'So where are we from then, Miss Ruth?'

I was scared. I had offended them. 'I don't know. I mean, I think of you guys as Americans.'

'Ruth. I have never lived there. I have been there five times.' Here, she held up a hand to my face with all of her fingers outstretched. 'I went there for my grandmother's funeral. We went a few times for the holidays, when my parents still lived here. And I went once to see my dad in the hospital. I haven't been back since. Five times.' She raised her outstretched hand again, to emphasise.

'So, you're from here? Like, if someone asks, you say you're Guatemalan?'

Carmen sighed and lay back down. 'Dwain, explain it to her.'

'I'm sorry, Carmen. I just don't get it,' I said.

'Forget it. No-one does,' Carmen said.

Dwain dropped the hose and turned it off at the tap and came to sit down with us.

He spoke to Carmen rather than me. 'You know, she's kind of right in a way.'

'In what way?'

'Well. We're not really from here.'

'So where are we from, Dwain? Are you American?'

'I don't know.'

'See,' she said. 'No-one knows. Our parents dumped us here.'

'That's not how it happened,' Dwain said, quietly.

'Okay, Dwain. You have your story. I'll have mine.' And Carmen put her sunglasses back on.

Dwain didn't look at me but went back to watering the lawn. No-one talked. I felt I shouldn't be there.

Carmen and Dwain were both in their own private thoughts now. We were quiet and I lay on my back and pretended to look at the sky. Dwain was sitting facing the lake, resting his hands on his knees, picking grass and throwing it away. Carmen was looking at the sky too, but I could tell she was really looking and that she was not pretending like me.

After a while, she spoke.

'Dwain?' Carmen said.

'What, Carmen?'

'Do you think we had a bad childhood?'

'I don't know. Ask Ruth.'

But they didn't ask me and I didn't say anything and when it got cold the mosquitoes came out and we went inside and made dinner. And the rest of the evening had the sadness of a Sunday night, even though it was only Saturday.

It took a long time to fall asleep that night. I woke up in the middle of the night. I thought I had heard a noise, someone trying to get in. I lay there and the night around me was quiet, and I thought that maybe the noise had been a dream.

I couldn't get back to sleep though. I lay awake and the room was hot and outside there was pale blue light. There must have been a full moon. I thought about Carmen and Dwain and what they had said that afternoon. I thought about their lives and how they couldn't seem to get going or attach to anything. I thought about my own life and for the first time in a long time I remembered that I was separate from them. My life was not like theirs, and I had come here for my own reasons that had nothing to do with them. I had forgotten about my own reasons in getting so caught up with them.

I got up and put a jumper on and went out to sit in the garden. It was sacred, sitting out there, alone in the garden and the moonlight. There, in the moonlight, I was meeting myself as though I was somebody else. It was like I was another person who had gone away and was now back. It was a reunion. I felt a tingling. The night was quiet and the quiet stretched out and it made me feel big and wide. The lake seemed like pure softness. *This*, I thought. *I came here to find this.* It was here. And I was close. I was just not close enough yet.

12

Something had been changing for me. It was to do with the boys, and the mother, and the way we went to the lake every day. It was to do with how peaceful our lives had become, and it was to do with the way I had felt that night in Jaibalito. I had gone in too strong with Carmen and Dwain; I had been too desperate, looking for a life, and now I had one, but I had forgotten about myself.

Carmen messaged me but I didn't reply. I would reply later. That night in Jaibalito had made me quiet inside and I did not feel like talking.

I don't know why I didn't reply to Carmen. I felt bad about it but when I tried to reply, I wrote something and then couldn't send it. I knew I would have to see her again, that it was only a matter of time, of course. We were friends. And I wanted to see her. But for now, I didn't want to talk to her and I didn't really know why.

I returned to my discipline of swimming every day, no matter how the weather was. I ate breakfast while sitting in my towel on the steps. I started taking the boys out earlier and coming back later and nobody seemed to mind and the boys enjoyed it and so did I. I got home late and the days tired me out. I didn't talk to anyone and I went to sleep early; I slept long and deep. I didn't cook anymore but ate queso fresco on bread; I drank coffee or ginger tea and sometimes I had an apple to feel healthy. Something was happening to me but I didn't know what, and it didn't seem to be coming from me.

In the past week Carmen had called and left two messages to which I had not responded. I would reply on the weekend, I had said to myself. On Thursday night, it started to rain and lightning lit up the sky. I had just come home from my day with the boys and I lit the stove with a match and blew the match out and I heard the back gate bang. I turned around and saw Carmen standing at my sliding glass door. She didn't knock but stood there with large bloodshot eyes. Her hair was dark and flat with rain and it stuck to the sides of her head. She wore a man's shirt and the same baggy brown pants that she was wearing the first time I saw her. She stood and watched me and waited for me to come and open the door.

She seemed like a ghost. I was afraid of her but I pretended not to be. I opened the door as if nothing was wrong. Carmen walked in and paced around the room like a tiger in a cage. She picked things up and put them down without looking at them.

I asked if she wanted tea. She was dripping rainwater on the floor where she walked. She almost opened the drawers but stopped herself and turned to face the room. I filled a saucepan with water and put it on the stove. I could smell the gas and I could hear it too, the rushing sound, of urgency. I asked her how she had been.

'Fine, you know.' She wrung her hands together and blew on them as she stared at the calendar on the wall. 'Your calendar is wrong. It's the right month but the wrong year.'

'I don't use it. It came with the house. It was here when I moved in.'

'Oh,' Carmen said, then started pacing again without looking at me. 'What else here isn't yours?' She said this as an accusation, which I ignored.

'Most of this stuff isn't mine. I only had my backpack when I moved in. I told you that when you first visited, remember?'

Carmen looked at me for the first time since she arrived. 'Why would I remember that? I have a life, you know.' She stared for a moment and then sat on the couch in her wet clothes.

'What kind of tea do you want?'

'I didn't say I wanted tea.'

I sighed. I turned the stove off and sat down next to her.

'Carmen.'

'Have your tea, Ruth.'

'Is this because I haven't called you back yet? I was going to call you this weekend. I've been busy with the boys.'

'Like I would give a shit. Ha. That's hilarious.' She threw her head back and laughed and she kept laughing for too long, drawing it out so long it was awkward. I wanted to sigh again and instead I stood up and relit the stove. I leant against the bench, looking at the floor. I put one of the teacups away. I felt Carmen watching me like an animal. She was waiting for me to talk. I suddenly felt very tired. I rubbed the bridge of my nose and closed my eyes.

I wasn't sure how much time had passed when Carmen stood up with a jolt.

'Have your fucking tea,' she yelled, and she walked out the door and slid it shut with a bang.

I didn't move. I stood in the kitchen for a long time after that. The rain had made the air very cold and I was not wearing enough clothes. The water was boiling and I turned off the gas. I poured hot water into the cup. My hands were shaking and some of the water spilled. I left the tea on the bench with the tea bag still in it and went to bed even though it was only seven-thirty. Twice that night I thought I heard someone at the door and I got up to check but no-one was there. I double-checked that I had bolted the door and fell asleep with the lights still on. I suddenly felt very far from home. Wherever home even was.

After that night when she appeared at my house, Carmen was moody. She disappeared often, for a couple of weeks at a time, and then she came back, fresh and happy, but false. In the time before she disappeared, she was glum and unhinged. When she came back she never said where she had been. Once I asked Dwain where she went.

He shrugged. 'To the city, I guess. To the underworld.' He put on a Halloween voice when he said this. He didn't say anything more and I knew the conversation was over. I didn't ask him again.

When Carmen returned, she brought me gifts. She never talked about what happened before she left, all the mean things she had said and done. The gifts were not expensive but they were thoughtful and sweet. Once, she gave me a leather backpack.

'For your hikes,' she said. 'They make these in Chichicastenango; they sew them by hand. See?' Carmen pointed to the stitching around the edge.

She came back smelling of the beach; her hair was the colour of sand. When I asked her about her time away, she waved her hand around and said, 'Oh, you know.' She wore wooden jewellery.

Each time she came back, she tried to start again, with the people in her life and with life itself. It was as though, while she was away, she had made promises to herself that now she was trying to keep. She went back to work and she worked every day. For a while she got up early and came with me on my swims.

One morning, when we got out of the water, she looked up towards the hill. 'This is great!' she said, as though surprised, as though she had never done this before, as though she had not spent her whole life here.

For a while she stopped going to El Nahual. I didn't know what she did but sometimes I saw her in the street, looking plain and clean, not dressed flamboyantly but ordinary and almost ugly, but not quite, wearing a men's navy corduroy shirt that she had bought to replace her old brown one. She walked with purpose and when she saw me she stopped and hugged me and then said she had to go and she kept on walking. She was full of calm and seriousness.

Sometimes on our morning swims she talked about how she would like to go to university; she told me about how once in Antigua she met a woman, an American, a university professor. The woman was a professor of anthropology and she came to Guatemala to do field work. She had been coming here since the seventies. The professor gave courses, in Guatemala City, courses in anthropology, and Carmen had always wanted to take one. Carmen talked about this on our morning swims; she talked about the courses and how she would do one and how maybe she would go to America and study anthropology, properly, in a degree. She had known someone who had done one of the courses in the city; he told her how at the start of each class the professor walked into the room with a can of Coke; she sat the Coke down on the desk and announced to the class, 'Let's begin.' After meeting the professor, Carmen had bought some books on Mayan anthropology and linguistics and other things. Carmen told me about how these days, after the swim, she went home to read her anthropology books; every morning before she began she took a can of Coke from the fridge and opened it and put it on the table and said, 'Let's begin.' She told this to me with an embarrassed laugh and rolled her eyes at herself.

These phases lasted for a few weeks. Sometimes longer. Phases of hard work and seriousness and future plans. Phases of taking herself seriously. Of not needing to be the centre of attention, of not partying. Phases of quiet, solitary mornings of concentration and trajectory. And then, slowly, it changed. Cracks appeared. Carmen came for the swim but she was late to arrive and she seemed annoyed at me. She no longer looked up at the hill as we emerged from the lake but she looked down at the sand, kicking cans with her toes.

'Fucking rubbish,' she said, scanning the beach. 'I'm sick of this place.' Her face was dark and dark circles appeared under her eyes. Her skin was pale and blotched.

Some days she didn't come swimming at all, then she missed three days in a row.

Then she was gone again for weeks and I hoped that she had gone to America, for university, like she had been talking about, or even Antigua, for the course.

Once, when Carmen started skipping the swims, I offered to help her with the university thing.

Carmen turned to look at me straight on. 'What, write my application or something? Like I'm ten years old? I can do it, you know. I'm not dumb. I am not your child. Stick to the boys.'

'I don't know. I could do some research, look things up. Do you know which university you want to go to? We could look up the requirements.'

'Of course I know which school I want to go to. The one that the professor teaches at. In Texas.'

Carmen stood on the sand and pulled her wet hair back and squeezed the water out. It dripped in patterns on the ground. 'I know what you think. You think I'm hopeless. You think I won't do it on my own. You think you're starting some kind of intervention program. You and Dwain, you're both the fucking same.'

She stepped close to me and I could see the lake water beading on her skin. 'I don't need your help. You're not even from here. What would you know, about anything? Concentrate on your own failed life, not mine.'

Carmen didn't come swimming after that and the next time I saw her was at El Nahual, wearing her blue kaftan.

Emilie and I still spoke on the phone, though not as often as we did before, when she had first started calling me. Our lives had become entwined in the places we were living. Emilie had made friends, we both had our work, and we didn't need each other like we did before. But we still spoke, and I still thought of her, but now in a friendly, far-off way. One night Emilie asked me if I wanted to visit her in Pátzcuaro.

'I don't know. Maybe. Yeah, no, that would be nice.' I paused. 'I'd love to. It's just the boys really. I'd have to see if I can get time off. Or wait until they go to the city next.'

'When's that?'

'Next month, maybe. I don't know.'

'Why don't you see if you can get time off?'

'I don't know if I can. The mum's never around. Who will look after the boys?'

'You have to take a break every now and then.'

'Let me check.'

On Thursday the boys and I came back to the house as usual after the afternoon at the lake. Mariella was in the kitchen, moving around. She seemed gloomy today. I moved to leave like I usually did, and Rafael rushed up to me and grabbed my hand. He pulled me down and he whispered in my ear, 'Please don't go.' Josue held my other hand tight without saying anything. Eduardo watched from the end of the kitchen bench, looking nervous and serious.

The mother appeared in the living-room doorway, holding a magazine. She was wearing make-up and she had done her hair and she wore gold hoop earrings. She smiled at us when she walked in. She was tall and strong as an athlete. She was alert, roused from the lethargy of the past few months. I had hardly seen her for months, and when I had, she had been wearing a robe and hadn't done her hair.

The two younger boys were still holding on to me.

'Boys, that's enough. Let her go.'

Josue took a small step even closer to me, watching his mother.

Rafael didn't move and he didn't let go of my hand. 'No,' he shouted, and I felt him squeeze my hand. 'I want her to stay. I don't care what you say.'

The mother strode towards us like a pointed arrow and grabbed each boy roughly by the wrist. They cried out and held on to me with their other hands. The mother yanked them hard and they both started to cry.

She looked at me icily. 'You can go now, Ruth. You can leave.'

It rained heavily that whole night and the rain kept falling into the next morning. It rained all morning and it was still raining when I left to go to work. The rain was heavy and tiring. The water beat heavily on my raincoat and drops fell down my face.

At the house, the mother was dressed again, and the blinds were open. Mariella ignored me. I searched for the boys, for the basket I always took to the lake.

The mother walked to me in a cloud of strong perfume that made her seem like an insect. She said I didn't need to pack today. She said I didn't need to take the boys out. She said there were a lot of small jobs to do and that she could take care of the boys so that I could get them all done. I could see Eduardo in the corner of the room. He was doing a puzzle. He didn't look at me. I felt lead in my feet. The mother poured a whiskey and sat down.

'Now,' I said, to no-one, really, trying to sound light and friendly. 'Let's see.' I picked up the list and I didn't know why but I made an exaggerated show of reading the jobs. Eduardo didn't say anything.

A week later the mother fired me. It happened quickly. She said she had needed the help before because she had not been well; she was feeling so much better now and she could manage on her own. She said Eduardo was going to boarding school in the city in a few weeks. She would just have the two younger ones then, and they spent half the day in school, anyway. I saw lipstick marks on her glass. She was leaning on one end of the bench and I saw her gold rings and her flaky skin and blue veins popping out. I heard Eduardo move in his room, but he didn't come out.

'You've been so very helpful over these last ten months.' The mother stared at me. She was sorry it was all so very last-minute, she said, with a mocking look. Today would be my last day, she said; I wouldn't need to come back again. I glanced at the two boys and I pushed back tears, desperate not to let the mother see. The mother walked out of the room; the kitchen was quiet and it smelled of her.

Rafael and Josue looked at me from the living room. Eduardo came out of his room. I turned to them and I gestured to the garden and they followed me. We walked to the back of the garden, by the fence, to the spot where you could see the lake.

I thought about what I might say to them. Their sadness felt worse than my own. I could not protect them from what lay ahead. It had already started. It had started long ago.

They stood by the fence and I held them, Rafael on my left and Josue at my right. Eduardo stood off to one side. I held the smaller ones tight and I told them I loved them and that I always would. I knew it would not be enough. And I knew they would forget.

The mother called us inside. She had prepared the snack that I usually made. While the children were eating, the mother watched me. I couldn't look her in the eyes. Finally, I left. I hugged their small bodies and then I walked out. It was done now. I was gone.

That night I went to drink in the cantina Carmen loved, the one by the lake with corrugated iron walls. There were long benches with shiny, peeling paint and the garden around the edges grew thick. Leaves reached in where people sat. It was mainly drunk men. I was tough now, and I felt old, and the drunk men left me alone. I had started to feel that this place was my home and now I knew that wasn't true. This place was not my home. I saw that now and I felt it too. The more I drank, the louder the feeling of loneliness got. Finally, I put coins in the jukebox and danced with the drunk men one by one. Then I went back up the hill to my house and I lay on the couch and I passed out.

13

Over the next few days, I dropped my routines. I went to El Nahual to hang out with the foreigners. I drank a lot of coffee and then I started drinking beer. And then, I saw Dwain.

He was walking up the hill and I was walking down, but when he saw me, he turned around and he walked along next to me. He rolled a cigarette and looked out into the hot sun as though he was looking over the whole day, and into the future too, and he said, 'Where we going, babe?'

His hair was longer than before and he walked with a swagger that was new. He had come over from Jaibalito for the weekend and he did not even have a bag. He seemed free. He seemed sad too though, and I wondered if that was part of it.

We went to El Nahual, and then to the cantina that I went to the other night, and then we decided to catch the last boat to Jaibalito. We had been drinking all day and it felt late. When I checked the time it was only five. The sun was still hot when we got on the boat. The water sounded cool. But I looked at the sky.

It felt strange to be going to Jaibalito with just Dwain. I had not been there without Carmen before. But now, as we caught the boat, with the wind, the feeling of drunkenness and Dwain with long hair and skinny and free, I hoped that Dwain would be alright. I don't know why I hoped for that but I did and when we got to the shore, I made a silent prayer. Carmen had disappeared again. I was worried about her. But I was glad to be here with Dwain.

That first night in Jaibalito we were too drunk to do anything much. Dwain put on a DVD from the collection stored in the cabinet underneath the TV. I sat on the couch with him for a while and drank tea. Then I felt tired and I went to bed and I didn't wake up until morning.

The morning felt like a different thing. I lay in the bed with the crisp white sheets. I listened to the morning sounds. The boats started up for the day. Miguel arrived and I heard him moving things in the back shed. Dwain woke up and got up and then he went back to bed. I heard a tap running, the toilet flushing. A phone vibrated in the next room.

For the first time since I had arrived at the lake I was happy to not be in my house. I was relieved to be here and I wanted to stay. I knew Dwain wouldn't mind. I knew I could stay here as long as I liked. I rolled onto my back and I listened to the sound the pillow made as I lifted my head and dropped it down again.

Dwain talked about Carmen in the morning. He thought she was probably in the city somewhere, but he didn't know.

'Why does she do that?'

'What, disappear? Could you stay in Panajachel your whole life and never leave? You have to get out from time to time if you live here. You'll see.'

'But it seems like more than just getting out. Like something kind of scarier.'

Dwain was quiet. I saw now that he had been acting before. He had been giving a speech that he had made many times. He had been protecting Carmen. He looked down and his hair fell forwards and he pushed it back with one hand and held it there.

'Yeah. That's true, in a way. It's when she can't cope. She goes there to kind of go crazy, because she can't let herself go crazy here.'

'You mean, like actually crazy?'

'Nah. She goes wild, you know? She hangs out with the party kids in the bars in Zone 2. The gay kids, the trans kids, the women who want to have lots of sex and who don't want to have to get married. The misfits. The ones who have been kicked out by their families. The poets too, the artists and the ones who are trying to talk about how fucked up their lives have been. Even all these years after the war, everyone's lives are still fucked up. Their parents went missing when they were little kids. That sort of thing. They live sort of close to the edge because they have nothing left to lose. Carmen goes to be with them. I went there a few times too. It was too much for me. They're intense. But they match Carmen perfectly. And they kind of protect her when she's there. Her nickname is "Queenie". They love her, like we all do. She goes there to go wild, and they let her, because they go wild too.'

'Is it safe?'

'What's safe? She's not safe here. There are more important things than safe. But they love her. They don't know her like we do. But they do love her there.'

I felt scared. I hadn't known it was that bad with Carmen. But maybe it wasn't that bad. Really, all Dwain had said was that she goes into the city to go partying for a little while. Everyone drinks, everyone lets loose. Dwain and I were drinking right now. Life is too hard to get through without having something like that. Maybe going to the city was helping her survive. I said this to Dwain.

He smiled gently. 'Yeah, maybe, Ruth. You're probably right. I'm sure you are.' We didn't talk about Carmen after that.

I stayed at Dwain's house and didn't think of going home. I didn't think about the family, I didn't think about my life. Every time thoughts of my life came up, I pushed them away, to the side, out of sight. I stayed in the spare room with dark wood and white walls and the room came to feel more like home than my house in Panajachel. I wondered for the first time if I should give it up. I wondered what I would do now that I had no job. One afternoon, after I had been there for a week, I was lying on the grass in the sun, almost asleep. I felt a vague sense of panic at what my life had become. I went to take a sip of coffee and the mug was empty and cold. I moved to sit up and make a new pot when I heard a shout behind me.

'You bitch! You're here!' I turned around and saw Carmen standing there, wearing sunglasses and a silk kimono over her baggy old jeans. Her hair was loose and shiny and I couldn't see her eyes. She stood with her arms stretched out and she smiled wide. There were several paper shopping bags at her feet. She wore a lot of silver bangles on one wrist and when she hugged me they jingled like a child's song.

I asked her where she had been this time and as usual she waved her hand around in the air and gave a vague response. I called Dwain and he came out and we took out everything that was in the fridge and had a feast. We had sliced tomatoes with olive oil, white cheese wrapped in waxed paper, fluffy bread that we broke into pieces, ham, slices of cheese. Carmen was happy. Dwain was happy. And I was happy too. Carmen didn't take her glasses off though, and when she took a sip of coffee, her hands shook.

With Carmen back, we settled into a routine, quiet like a family. We had breakfast together and then we went for a walk and in the afternoons we watched old DVDs, sometimes talking the whole way through, sometimes watching silently.

Carmen talked about university. Dwain talked about Jaibalito, the house, the things Miguel was teaching him. I was quiet and tried to think what I would do but I didn't know so I didn't say anything.

In the mornings I lay in bed a long time. I looked out at the garden, not wanting to get up. I got up when I heard Carmen in the kitchen. By now I could tell who it was from the specific sounds that they made.

I walked into the kitchen and Carmen was there, moving around, making coffee and humming. She was wearing the same dark kimono over her sleeping clothes that she had been wearing the day she came back. She was fresh. She smiled at me.

'Heya, Ruthie.' She held up a mug and raised her eyebrows at me, offering me coffee without saying anything. I nodded.

We were quiet as she made the coffee. I walked through the living room and looked outside. The day was bright. An aeroplane flew overhead and it left a single white line. Then Carmen was behind me, holding a tray, and she pointed to the garden with her chin.

Outside, Carmen took off her kimono and lay it on the grass that was still wet from the morning. She placed the tray on top of it. We sat down, cross-legged, facing each other. Carmen poured the coffee. I smelled the steam.

We were quiet as we sipped. We were both in our thoughts. Out of nowhere, I thought of the Camino de Santiago. I had always wanted to do it and I thought of it now. It was to do with the day, the coffee, the clear sun, the smell of grass, being outside in the morning. I remembered I had wanted to do it.

I turned to Carmen. 'Have you ever wanted to do the Camino?' Already I knew that I shouldn't have asked. Even when I was asking, I knew what her answer would be.

'That's for tourists.'

'Yeah, but, Carmen, it's in Spain. Even you would be a tourist in Spain.'

'No I wouldn't. Not like that. Being a tourist has nothing to do with where you're from. It's all in here.' Carmen tapped her head aggressively. She almost seemed like she was going to cry.

I knew what she meant. It was a certain way to live. Some of us were tourists. Most of us were, most of the time.

Carmen looked at me, about to say something, then shook her head and bit her lip and laughed away the last thing she had said. We drank our coffee. I played with the grass. But I felt strong. I was determined today.

'Isn't there anything that you actually want to do? Why do you dismiss everything? You just brush everything away. We all have to do something in life. A lot of things, actually. Life is long. We need to pass the time. What's wrong with the Camino? I think it would be nice.'

'Ruth, if you want to do the Camino, do the Camino. But that shit is not for me.'

'But that's my point. Nothing is for you. You reject everything. You hate it all. Is there nothing you think would be worthwhile to do?'

Carmen bit her lower lip and was quiet for a long time. She picked up her cup and ran it along the grass, moving it around in small circles.

Finally she spoke. Her voice was soft. 'Why is this never enough? Why do people always need to improve their shitty lives? Everyone's lives are shitty, why are they trying to get away? They take trips, do other things. I like being here in Jaibalito, just sitting on the grass, with you. Drinking coffee. Dwain inside, asleep. The lake down there, the dumb little waves falling at the shore. Why is this not enough?'

Carmen's answer was something I did not expect and with Carmen being soft and pensive like this, I felt more like Emilie, always looking for other things. At the start of the conversation I had felt like the wise one; now it was the other way around. I didn't say anything. I finished the coffee and played with my mug, tipping it over and straightening it up again. I heard Dwain moving around inside.

Carmen spoke again. 'But hey, Ruth, you're right too. You know, we do need to do stuff to fill in the time.' She was being generous. It made her seem normal. 'Yeah. I should do something, shouldn't I? Get a real job, study something.'

'I think what you said was beautiful, Carmen.'

'Yeah, I know. But I forget about the world I am actually living in.'

I knew what she meant, because I felt it too, and I had never heard anyone else say it before. I looked at her and I wanted to cry. She didn't fit here. She didn't fit anywhere. Her hair hung over to one side. She shone on the lawn in the morning sun.

As though she could read my mind, she pushed me playfully. 'You big fool.' She cocked her head to one side. 'Is that Dwain? About time. For Christ's sake. It must be like eleven or something.' It was only nine-thirty but I didn't tell her that.

14

Emilie had called me a few times since I had been fired. I had not answered the phone and I hadn't texted her back. The following day, in the afternoon, when Carmen was making a meal and Dwain was in the garden shed, I walked to the jetty and I called her.

She didn't answer but she rang back not long after. I had gone inside to help Carmen with the food. I went out into the garden and answered the phone. Emilie started talking without waiting for me to say hello.

'You called. I'm glad. I was starting to wonder what was going on.'

I told Emilie everything, about being fired and coming to Jaibalito and staying for two weeks. She asked me questions and listened to the answers. After being with Carmen and Dwain, Emilie felt like a stranger now. I couldn't explain. It felt like an effort to talk to her. I had to pretend.

'You're in Jaibalito? How long have you been there?'

I had already told her but I told her again.

'And what are you doing? I mean, what are you going to do?'

I told her that I didn't know, and that I was thinking about giving up my house in town. She was silent.

'Why don't you come here?'

'What, Pátzcuaro?'

'Sure. Why not?'

'What would I do there?'

'The same thing that you would do anywhere. Just live.'

I didn't know if she was being wise or facetious. I didn't want to go to Pátzcuaro. I didn't want to leave here. Maybe if she had asked me before. I didn't care what Carmen said. I had found family here. I hadn't thought that would happen for me. But it had happened, and now I wanted to keep it. I felt cool, cut off from Emilie.

'I don't know. I'm actually thinking about moving here.' I had not been thinking about moving to Jaibalito, but as soon as I said it, I knew it was true.

'What, and live with Carmen and Dwain?'

'Carmen doesn't live here, she lives in Panajachel. I wouldn't live with Dwain. No. I don't know. Maybe I could find my own place. A little house somewhere. I don't know.'

As soon as I said it I knew that it was what I wanted to do. When I got off the phone I walked inside and sat at the kitchen bench. I felt light.

Carmen was mixing up salad dressing in a jar. She glanced at me. 'What are you so happy about?'

'Nothing.'

Carmen was looking back down, screwing the lid on the jar and then she started shaking it. 'Was that your girlfriend?'

'She's not my girlfriend.'

'Whatever.'

'Carmen? I love you.'

Carmen paused for a second and then kept shaking the jar. 'Fuck off.'

'I do. I love you. I've never had a friend like you before.'

She hesitated and sniffed, then she tossed her head. 'Well. I'm not saying it back.'

'Okay.'

Carmen looked up at me, surprised, and then she laughed. She seemed so ordinary, and very real. I had not seen her laugh like that before. Plain, from within.

'You're an idiot, Ruth.' She opened the jar and dabbed dressing on my nose. But she was smiling on the outside and also underneath.

I went back to my house in Panajachel and met my landlady and gave notice on my lease. Over the next few weeks I started sorting through my things. I knew I would need help to find a job and a house. I arranged to meet with Dwain.

I met him on a Saturday morning. Carmen had become serious and studious again and he was staying at her house but she did not want to come out. We met for breakfast. Everything felt easy, suddenly.

We sat at a table on Santander, outside, in the sun. There were market stalls on both sides of the street, just up from where we were. There were people from the city, couples in cream pants and sunglasses, looking at the stalls and heading for the lake.

I ordered coffee and eggs and refried beans. Dwain had coffee and smoked cigarettes. I drank the coffee quickly and asked for more. I ate all of the tortillas that came in a basket wrapped in cloth.

Dwain was amused. 'My, my, the life has come back to you. Next thing you know you'll be having sex.'

I rolled my eyes. 'We all know *that* won't be happening.'

He threw his head back and laughed and crossed one leg over the other and rested his hands on his lap. Dwain was very beautiful this morning, relaxed and dignified.

I told Dwain all about my plan, how I wanted to move to Jaibalito. I told him I needed help to find a house and a job. He smiled, nodding, imagining things. He reached out and squeezed my shoulder and gave it a rub.

'Well, Ruth, we'd love to have you. Remember Miguel? He knows everyone. I'll ask him.'

And I was surprised at his answer even though I had asked.

The following week I got a message from Dwain. 'Come and see me when you can. I have an update.'

I went to Jaibalito the next day. I was nervous. I had already given notice on my house in a fit of belief that things would work out. Now I really hoped that they would.

Dwain didn't come and meet me at the boat. He didn't do that anymore and that felt good. Already, stepping off the boat and onto the land and setting off alone with my small backpack, walking up the hill with the lake water at my back, it felt as though I lived here. I knew now that it would work out. That I would move to Jaibalito. That somehow, it would work out.

I crossed the empty allotment to get to Dwain's house from the main path. There were five crows feeding in the empty land. One jumped up on the fence as I approached. One flew into a tree. The one in the tree called out as I passed. It sounded like a baby.

Dwain had just woken up when I arrived. He was in the kitchen making breakfast. He seemed very tired and when I opened the glass door, he looked up and smiled wearily. He made an effort to be friendly and welcoming, and it worked. But I could see that it was an effort.

Dwain sat at the small table just outside the door. I made tea and went outside to sit with him. He sprinkled hot sauce over his eggs and licked it off his fingers. The sauce had run down the side of the bottle and formed a ring on the table. He looked agitated when he saw the ring. I remembered when I first met him and what I thought he was, with the greasy hair and the flannelette shirt. He was not that, actually, underneath.

Dwain ate his eggs and talked to me between mouthfuls of food.

'So, I spoke to Miguel. He's kind of a big deal in this town, and he knows everyone. I thought either he or his wife might be able to help. So I asked him and at first he didn't say anything. I thought I had upset him or something. But he came back way later, like, just yesterday, and told me had spoken to some people and they have worked something out for you. It's kind of like that here. When I first asked him, he asked all sorts of questions about you. He remembers you from seeing you here, but he asked all about you. I wasn't sure what he thought. And you're a foreigner. Anyway, they must have decided that you're okay and they're happy to have you live here, because he came back and said he had found an empty hut that you could use, and that you can work at the school.'

I felt excited and happy and nervous too. 'I didn't realise what a big deal it would be.'

'That's the way it is here, babe. This is not Panajachel. You can't just come and be a tourist here.'

Dwain finished his eggs and arranged his knife and fork neatly on his plate and lifted up the sauce bottle again and put it on his plate. He wet his finger and rubbed away the ring the sauce had made.

'Yeah. So there is one thing, though, about moving here. Miguel told me yesterday. The school can't actually pay you. They don't have any money to employ anyone new. So he's talking to the villagers to try and figure it out. I don't know what they'll come up with.' He breathed. 'But I bet they come up with something.'

I was getting nervous now. Already I could see that this was going to be different from Panajachel. I was going to have to be part of the community. I had not been part of a community for so long.

Dwain pushed his plate back and rolled a cigarette.

'We'll go and chat to him later. Okay? We'll see what he says.' He breathed out a cloud of smoke.

'Okay,' I said. I moved in my chair and looked out at the view. I breathed out a sigh.

I looked at Dwain. Dwain looked back at me. There were wrinkles around his eyes.

'It'll be great to have you here, Ruth. I hope it works out.'

'Me too,' I said. But I was scared.

We went to see Miguel that afternoon. It was hot and dry and had not rained in weeks. I had always thought of Dwain as a foreigner. But he was born here and he had grown up here and this was his home. I could see it now for the first time as he walked through the narrow paths between the tall fences of the vegetable plots, walking strong in his long shorts, with brown calves and brown feet, walking flat and straight and firm like any village boy.

Miguel was sitting outside his house on a wooden stool, to the side of the door. His wife was inside, putting wood in the stove. I could see through the door that inside was small and dark, with low ceilings. The wife was mumbling to herself.

Miguel rose when he saw us and he reached for my hand. He held my hand in both of his hands and looked into my face. He spoke softly. 'You are welcome here.' He released my hand and his wife brought two more stools and Miguel gestured to us both to sit down. His wife handed us each a small cup of coffee and then she stood in the entrance to the hut and watched us talk.

Miguel spoke first. 'Dwain tells me that you would like to move to Jaibalito.'

I nodded but I didn't speak.

'He tells me you're a teacher of English. That's good. We can use an English teacher here.'

I nodded again, even though I was not technically a teacher. I swallowed and tried to hide it. I heard the chickens in the back courtyard.

'I've made enquiries. It's difficult. But we can arrange something. We can set something up for you.'

Dwain was quiet and so was I. Next to Miguel, I felt flighty. He was solemn. He had thought things through.

'Dwain might have told you this already – there's no money at the school. They cannot employ someone new. Dwain said you would be happy to live simply.'

I glanced at Dwain. He didn't look at me. I was confused. I had thought that I had chosen to move here of my own free will. Now it felt as though this place was choosing me.

'There is a hut. It's small and very basic. But it's close to the school and it's empty now, and the owner has children in the school. He is happy for you to live there. You don't need to pay.'

I nodded and smiled. My mouth was dry. I felt awkward. Dwain was listening.

'There are other costs associated with living. The water is provided by the town. We all take our jugs and fill them at the tap. You can do that too.' He paused and took a sip from his cup and he glanced back towards the room. 'And please, when you need something, come and ask. Don't be shy.'

Miguel finished talking now and I could feel that it was time for me to say something. I felt strange, trapped and touched all at the same time.

'I am grateful to you and the town. I will be sure to do my best.'

Miguel smiled and put down his cup. He reached out his hand, just one hand this time. He shook my hand and nodded at me. Then he said, 'Welcome to Jaibalito, Ruth.'

On the way back to the house, I asked Dwain what he thought. He laughed. He put his arm around me as we walked.

'Don't freak out, babe. This is just how they do things here. It doesn't mean anything. All the foreigners around here volunteer. They're used to it.'

The sun was setting right in front of us. We walked in silence the rest of the way.

The next few weeks were flurried and strange. I packed up my house, which didn't take long. I gave away a few of my things, and the rest I put in boxes. Aside from that, I did the usual things. But I couldn't wait to leave.

I had told Carmen about my plans. She was delighted. But she didn't understand why I didn't just live with Dwain. 'He's basically family,' she said.

'I like to be alone.'

'You won't be alone. You'll be at Dwain's all the time.'

I didn't say anything.

'Suit yourself, weirdo,' she said.

But over the next few days Carmen helped me pack and clean my house and she came with me to the market to get a few extra things that I would need.

On my last night in Panajachel, she cooked me dinner and we drank red wine.

'To your new life,' she said. I raised my glass.

15

JAIBALITO AT NIGHT WAS PITCH black. It was so dark that it didn't make any difference whether you closed your eyes or you opened them – everything was dark. My hut had no electricity and I had a camp stove for cooking. I used a candle at night for light.

I went to bed early that very first night. I lay awake for a long time. I could hear all the sounds of the night, sticks breaking, dogs barking, at first far away and then nearby. I didn't sleep for a long time, and then, it was morning.

The morning was clear and calm and warm. The neighbours were outside in their yard and when I opened my door they stood up and looked at me, curious and shy. I was tired from not sleeping that night. There were soft morning sounds of a group of women talking further down the road and there was the slow movement of the village coming alive. I made coffee on my camping stove, bringing it out to the small porch and sitting on the wooden stool. I poured the coffee into my tin cup and walked to the place just beneath the tall tree where you could see a small glimpse of the lake.

The hut that had been loaned to me was on the side of the village next to the school. It was a very simple one-room hut made of mudbrick, with a swinging wooden door. There was a small porch of concrete just outside and an old wooden stool. There was an area of land in front of it, with two large avocado trees, and ripe avocadoes dropped to the ground. In the mornings I walked around the plot of land, picking up the ones that had fallen.

The day I started at the school, the children ran up to me and hid behind each other, giggling. The principal welcomed me formally. He showed me around the school, which was a small building with six or eight rooms. It was long and thin and painted yellow and had a dark-green roof. There was a soccer field in front of the school and beyond that was the lake.

The principal said the students were learning Spanish at school. Most spoke Kaqchikel at home. Some spoke Spanish at home as well. He told me they were glad the children would practise English with me. He said it would give them opportunities. I told him I was glad to be there. When I said it, I meant it, and I felt as though I was sitting on top of my life rather than off to one side.

The principal showed me a room at the back of the school. It had a few tables and chairs stacked up on one side and a chalkboard at the front. This was where I would give my English classes. On my first day, I cleaned up the room and arranged the furniture in a circle and found more desks and chairs. The other teachers had arranged my schedule and each period when the small bell rang, a new group of students appeared at my door. They were shy and unsure. Each period, five students arrived, grouped by year level. By the end of the week I had seen each group twice. The boys wore old t-shirts that were too big, tucked into their pants, with belts. The girls wore Kaqchikel dress: an embroidered blouse and a long straight skirt. Their hair was long and smooth and tied neatly in a braid.

I made an effort not to get to know the children or to develop any special relationships. I loved them as one whole group, rather than individually. I prepared one lesson every day and the lesson for each group was the same. I had five lessons every day and then I went home, or I went to Dwain's.

On the Friday afternoon after I started at the school, I went swimming down at the jetty. There were men on the shoreline who watched me swim and they watched as I got out and wrapped myself in a towel. There were children there too who I had seen at the school and they giggled as I dried my hair. This was not Panajachel. I didn't go swimming again.

Instead, I walked. When I was not with Carmen or Dwain, I walked up and around and over the hills. I walked to the top of one hill where you could see the whole lake and even beyond it. I found a small track on the side of the hill that led to the next village; I saw women or their daughters and sons walking this path with loads of vegetables.

When I didn't walk, I was at Dwain's. We ate together, we watched TV. I took a book from his shelf, which I kept next to the bed, and I read it every time that I slept there. When Carmen came it was different; we drank and we talked and we moved around a lot more. We went down to the lake and hung our legs off the jetty. I thought of Emilie. I should call her, I thought.

I had last spoken to Emilie when I had just been fired and had not yet moved to Jaibalito. Since then we had been messaging, but we had not spoken again. She was working on a big project now, doing interviews with the Purépecha women in the mountain towns. She had several students working for her. She was spending a lot of time in the mountains, and we didn't get much chance to talk.

One evening that I was not with Carmen and Dwain, I walked to the lake to call her. I sat on the edge of the jetty. It was late enough that everyone had gone home, but it was not dark yet. The air was still and very warm. The water lapped at the rotting wood; the jetty was old, and it creaked. I called Emilie and she didn't answer and I put my phone away. I sat and looked around. I didn't feel like going back home. The lights of Panajachel were coming on. A boat was travelling towards San Pedro. I thought of my house, of who was living in it. I was glad to be here now.

A few days later, Emilie called me back. She had been in the mountains when I rang and now she was back in Pátzcuaro. She asked me about Jaibalito. I told her about the school. She seemed impressed and she asked questions about my work. I did not tell her about Carmen and Dwain and how much time we were spending together, and what we did.

Dwain always had things to do to maintain the condition of the house. He was trying to learn to be handier and Miguel was teaching him. It was slow and he made a lot of mistakes. Carmen was idle when she was at Jaibalito. She worked at the café during the week, and she hated it. She was glum whenever I asked about it, so I didn't ask. She cooked a lot. She lazed in the sun. She smoked a lot of weed. So did Dwain. We all drank.

One night as we were on Dwain's back lawn, Carmen stood up. She said she wanted to go to the lake. Dwain rolled a joint and we took a bottle of wine and we walked there in bare feet. We sat on the jetty, all facing the same way. Carmen and Dwain smoked. Night fell.

From where we sat, we could see Panajachel. It was the same place I had sat when I phoned Emilie. It was the same time of day as well, and the lights of Panajachel were coming on, one by one, like stars in the sky. Dwain hung his head and watched the water below.

Carmen gazed towards Panajachel. 'The only thing I like in Panajachel is hanging out at El Nahual. That's really the only thing. And I don't even need that anymore. We have each other. We have Ruth. Look at us.' She waved a hand around. 'Isn't this better than El Nahual? It's our own little version of it.'

Dwain was quiet, his head still down. I didn't say anything. I didn't know what she meant. What was she talking about?

'I'm actually even thinking that one day I could leave. Be like you, Dwain. Come and go. Go to America.'

I looked at her and she looked back, fresh and new as a child.

Dwain spoke. 'I think you should. Pana is too small for you. You should get out. See if there's something more than this.'

'Yeah,' Carmen said, though she wasn't listening now. She was staring hard at Panajachel, as though she was planning something. She had a faint smile, so faint that it was barely there at all.

The next morning I went to the school as usual. I had drunk too much with Carmen and Dwain and I felt uneasy when I remembered what Carmen had talked about. About leaving. I wanted her to leave, of course; I could see how unhappy she was. But I felt uneasy. I wondered if it was the wine. I always felt anxious the day after wine.

I had stayed at Dwain's house the night before and on the way to the school I stopped at home and changed. I collected a bucket of water from the tap that I shared with the neighbours on both sides. I washed my face. The water was icy cold. There was mist on the lake.

At school the girls were wearing thick wool cardigans. The boys wore the same thin clothes as usual, and they shivered. The boys looked small. The girls looked old.

I sat in my room and prepared for the day. The school had no photocopier and I wrote exercises on the blackboard, which the students copied down. This week we were doing 'Animals'. Next week the theme would be 'Household Things'.

The children had started to say hello to me as I walked around the school. They ran up to me in groups, pushing their friends in front, and one brave student said in English, 'Hello,' saying the 'h' in the Spanish way, coarse like rocks and wind. Then they giggled and ran away. Later it became, 'Hello, how are you,' which they said like a statement, not a question. They ran off without waiting for a reply.

On Friday night, I went to Dwain's like I always did. I had been in Jaibalito for two months now, and I had a routine. I walked to his house the usual way, between my house and the neighbours', where there was a narrow path covered with gravel and stones. The sun was low and orange light came though the sparse trees. Music from the church started up. In front of me a woman was walking down to catch a boat. She had a load on her back and her sandals slapped on the ground as she walked.

Carmen was already at Dwain's when I arrived and it seemed like they had been waiting for me. Carmen was sitting at the table in the dining room, flipping through a magazine. She closed it when I opened the door and she turned to me.

'She's here,' Carmen called out to another room, and Dwain came out of his bedroom, all rumpled and half asleep.

Carmen looked at both of us. 'What should we do? Should we go down to the jetty?'

I thought about the jetty and how all we ever did there was drink and I thought about how I didn't want my students to see me there, drinking beer, and I didn't want the parents to see me either. I didn't want anyone else to see me who might tell someone who worked at the school, and when I really thought about it, I didn't want to go at all, even if no-one saw me. My life was changing, and I didn't want to sit around and drink beer anymore. I wanted to talk about other things. I wanted to read books. I wanted to learn new things.

'I don't know. Why don't we watch a movie instead?'

Carmen almost rolled her eyes at me, but she agreed and both she and Dwain drank beer and got stoned while we watched. When the movie ended, I went home.

I spent the next weekend alone. I had told Carmen and Dwain I wouldn't be visiting them. They didn't argue but I was worried I had hurt their feelings or that they would visit unannounced.

I didn't do anything very much, except sit around and arrange my things and make coffee and listen to the wind. In doing nothing, I was reminded of other things. I felt as though my compass was being reset. I loved Carmen and Dwain. They had opened my life to me. But now I wanted other things.

By Sunday afternoon, a sadness had landed on me like a mist. The sadness was wide and gentler than most things and I realised throughout that day that sadness wasn't such a bad thing.

I went to bed when it got dark, but I wasn't tired yet, and I lay awake. I remembered a sign I had seen on a noticeboard advertising a carving course. I had taken a photo of the sign, though at the time I didn't really know why. Lying awake in the dark, I remembered the course, and now I wanted to do it. It felt urgent. I couldn't sleep. I got out of bed and I looked up the dates. There was one in Antigua, starting in four weeks. I enrolled right there, and I was too energised to go back to sleep. I walked to the jetty and stood in the dark. I heard the water. I felt the cool air. There was a movement in the reeds, and a splash, and then it was quiet again.

I had thought about Emilie that weekend too. I thought about her much more than before, and in a different way. Before, I had wanted her to be in love with me. Now, I wanted her to be proud of me. I checked each action that I did against my internal imprint of her to see if she would approve. Emilie was living in the real world. I needed to live there too. Her life was working. I wanted mine to work too.

I saw there were two ways of being in the world. There was Carmen's way, and there was Emilie's. Both ways were inside me and I had to choose. It was obvious. The only way that worked was Emilie's. Carmen was beautiful and dysfunctional. In the past I had wanted to be more like her. Now, I needed to be like Emilie.

Emilie and I still spoke on the phone, though less than we did when I lived in Panajachel. We were both busy with our lives, and the heat and uncertainty that had been there at the start was gone and now we were more like family. When we spoke, I was surprised at how different she was, the Emilie on the phone from the Emilie of my thoughts. But I had been right; I told Emilie about my life, and she asked questions, and she was proud.

By the end of that week I had arranged with the school to take leave for the carving course. I told Carmen and Dwain when

I saw them that Friday. Dwain looked sad but happy for me too, in a gentle way.

Carmen rolled her eyes and she turned to Dwain. 'The poor thing, she still thinks there is something out there to find. When will she learn? This is all there is, right here.'

Dwain did not say anything. He looked at me and his eyes were sad, but his eyes said, *Go. Go for it.*

16

Antigua felt like a different world. There was a clean structure here that was not in Panajachel. There were cafés with signs in English advertising pizza and movie nights. There were well-maintained colonial buildings painted yellow and creamy white. There were tiny footpaths that ran alongside the buildings, which were right on the street. The market was undercover and orderly; there were no chickens or candles like in Panajachel, but stalls with neat piles of clothes and jewellery with labels written in English. The stallholders here spoke English too.

The hotel where I stayed, which had been recommended by the woman from the carving course, was just as lovely as the rest of the town, with its own internal patio with thick, dark-green tropical plants and white plastic tables and chairs. Every afternoon it rained very hard and the patio came alive. After the rain, it became very still, with wet ground and wet plants and a resting feeling; the fallen rain turned into steam.

The course was held in a large workshop in a building behind the marketplace. To get there you needed to push through wide wooden doors into a tiled corridor, then cross the internal patio to the other side, where there were two rooms. The room on the left was a ballet studio; the room on the right was the workshop, and this was where the carving class was held.

On the first day of the course, we sat in two rows like children on their first day of school. There were twelve of us who had enrolled, mainly foreigners, but there were two Guatemalans from the city. The rest of the class was from somewhere else: Argentina, Chile, Italy and Spain. There was a person from France and there was an American, who didn't say he was from America but called himself Alaskan instead; he told us they were two different things. Most of the others had carved before and were here to learn the local techniques. I was the only one who had not.

Class started each morning at eight. The teacher was a woman with rough grey hair tied back in a loose bun. Her hair was a mixture of silver and brown and her skin was luminous. She told us that her father was French and her mother was Kaqchikel; her face looked French and she wore Kaqchikel dress. She had studied carving in Mexico, in Argentina and in Spain, in Algeria and in France too. Every morning she came into the classroom carrying a set of tools. She put the tools down on the desk at the front and looked at each one of us one by one and she said, 'Everyone ready?' with an authority that made us afraid, even though we were adults and just doing the course for fun.

Over the course, she taught us carving techniques and how to work with the main types of tools. She showed us techniques from the different places she had been. But mainly she taught us the Guatemalan technique, since that was what she was learning now, and what she was most interested in. During class in the morning, she showed us what to do; after a break at noon we spent the afternoons on our own, in the workshop, practising. Each day was the same and the course ran for two weeks, with one day off on the Sunday.

At the end of each day, I was tired in a way that felt like charcoal, as though something inside me had been alight and now was all burnt up. It was different from the tired I felt after a day at the school. That one felt like I'd given something away that I needed and would have to grow back. The charcoal feeling made me peaceful and I wasn't thinking as much. I wasn't worrying about the future and my place in it, and I wasn't thinking about how I had failed at my life. Those things were no more or less true than before, but I wasn't thinking them now. That was what the carving was doing to me.

In the evenings, I sat in my room with the window open to the patio. There was hardly anyone in the hotel. I tried to practise what we had learnt that day. I felt wide inside and, for the first time, I did not miss anyone or even feel alone. Usually I missed someone who didn't even exist. I had been wanting to feel complete my whole life and I felt it then, in my hotel room with the courtyard air that smelled of rain and earth. I had always thought I needed something else, something specific that would cure me, when maybe all I needed was just to not think.

On the last day of the course I went out with the class for pizza and for beer. I drank red wine and with the altitude I became dizzy and left early. I went to my room and lay on my bed and scanned myself to see if I had changed. I realised now that I wanted my life to change and that is why I had enrolled in the course. I felt ashamed. A carving course couldn't change your life. I stayed in Antigua for three more days and did all the tourist things, and then I caught the bus to the city and from the city, back to the lake.

I got back on a Saturday. I immediately went to see Dwain. He was not home. I cleaned up my hut and I walked around. I walked home and sent a message to Carmen.

'I'm back,' I said.

She replied straight away. 'We are in Pana. Come over!'

I went to Panajachel that afternoon.

That week I tried to keep practising, practising carving and what it did to my mind. I practised in the evenings after school. On Thursday, Dwain stopped by my place and he said that Carmen hadn't been feeling well. He thought we should do something for her. He thought making pizzas might help. We did it that Friday night.

Carmen rolled her eyes. 'Guys. I am actually from here you know. I am not American. And anyway, pizza is from Italy.' But her cheeks were pink and she was happy with the attention we were giving her.

The following week Carmen disappeared again and by now I knew what I needed to do. I had my work. I taught at the school, and I carved. I bought groceries and I cooked and I cleaned. I felt satisfied. I did not drink or even think about it.

A few weeks later though, Dwain called and told me that Carmen was in a city hospital, and would I go and visit her.

They had found her in the city, in a share-house with poets and artistic types. The poets got scared when Carmen started acting strange and they called Dwain, who told them he would be there the next day.

I caught the bus up from the lake. Carmen was in a hospital in Zone 10. I caught a bus there from my hotel in Zone 2. On the avenida on the way there, there was dust and shouting and lines of stalls that sold phone covers and plastic toys. In Zone 10 the streets were hollow and strange, futuristic in a way, with tall buildings and high tinted windows. The cars that drove by were tinted too.

Carmen's room was on the fifth floor. It was a building like an office block, with tall windows and city views. The city below was very far down. You couldn't hear anything from outside. I followed a nurse down the long blue hall and her shoes squeaked on the shiny floor. The corridor was empty and spotlessly clean. Each room had a tiny window in the door and I saw flashes of the people inside. The nurse swiped a card and the door beeped twice and the nurse opened it and walked away.

Carmen was sitting on a chair by the window with her feet up on the seat. Her hair was long and seemed freshly washed and she was wearing a pale-blue hospital gown. I thought she looked beautiful, serene like water. She turned away from the window and looked towards the door when she heard me come in.

'You came,' she said softly, smiling from deep inside. 'I knew you would. Here, sit.' Carmen didn't get up from her chair but pointed to the neatly made bed. Aside from the hospital furniture and Carmen's gown, it could have been a hotel.

'How are you, Carmen? How are you feeling?' I watched her closely.

Carmen laughed. Her laughter sounded musical, like bells on a bracelet of a woman who danced. 'You know, I actually feel great. Sort of, free or something, you know? I don't know what happens. First I crack up, and then I am free. I wish I could feel like this all the time.'

I sat quietly. I didn't know what to say. She did seem free. I felt somehow that I should be disapproving of her, that I should instruct her in some way, tell her the right way to live. That I shouldn't 'encourage her', as people say. But I didn't know what to say. We sat in comfortable silence, as if we were alone, on a porch, on a summer's night.

I looked out the window. 'That's nice,' I said, pointing to the view outside. 'Do you miss the lake?'

Carmen rolled her eyes. 'The lake. The lake. Everyone loves the lake. The lake sucks you in. You can't get away.' She turned to look at me. 'Do you know what I've been thinking? I've been thinking about how the only way Americans leave the lake is by going crazy. Think about it, it's true. They wait and they wait and then they go mad and they get sort of jettisoned out. Don't you find that strange? You wouldn't think it, but it's true. It happened to my parents. And there's loads of others like them too. It's like there's some kind of dark magic there. Like it casts a spell, or it's a black hole.'

I didn't want to agree with her. I was supposed to be helping her sort out her life. How could Carmen be right, when she was the one in the hospital gown? And yet I found that I agreed with her. That Carmen was speaking the truth.

I changed the subject. 'Who brought you here?'

'Simon and Geraldo took me to Emergency. Then they called Dwain and Dwain called my mum. Or the other way around. Or something. My mum called my uncle and he arranged for me to come here.'

'How long will you stay? What will you do next?'

'Too many questions, little Ruth. Who cares? It's all the same. It doesn't matter where I am. Do you want some water?' Carmen unwrapped a paper cup and filled it with water from a jug. The sound of the water falling in the cup filled the whole room. There was no other sound.

I remembered the first time I went to Carmen's house and how Carmen made us plates of quinoa with olive oil and salt. Carmen sighed and looked out the window again. She seemed saner than she had ever been.

'My uncle lives in Texas. In Austin. He wants me to go back there with him.' She laughed and turned to look at me. 'He hates it here, you know. Like, he hates the whole country. He blames the country for what happened to my parents. And for what he thinks is happening to me. He thinks this country makes people crazy. He doesn't get it. It's the crazy ones who come here in the first place. They just make sure they come here before the crazy comes out, and then they stay here as long as they can while it all comes out. Then it comes out too much and someone has to come and take them home. That's how it happens, all the time.'

Afterwards I wasn't sure of anything. I walked back to the hotel. It was dark but it was early still, and the air was very warm. The streets were quiet and the people had gone home. I thought of Carmen in her hospital room, looking over the city as the night came on. I knew Carmen had seen something the world wanted to deny. I wondered how Carmen would survive knowing it. I wondered what it meant for my own life.

17

When Carmen came out of hospital, she came back to Panajachel. She stayed at home and she didn't take trips, not even to Jaibalito. Dwain had gone to the city and then the States, saying he would be gone just a couple of weeks. I stayed in Jaibalito and lived a sober life. I worked at the school and I took it seriously. Since I no longer saw Carmen and Dwain, in the evenings I practised what I had learnt at the carving course. I made small figurines from off-cuts of wood that they kept for me at the school. I made figurines and I hated them and sometimes I threw them into the lake. They were only practice, anyway.

Since her time in hospital, Carmen had changed. She was shaken. She no longer dressed flamboyantly or acted in loud ways; she no longer went to El Nahual. It was almost as though she was afraid of herself. And she was no longer sarcastic or even mean the way she could sometimes be. I visited her every Saturday.

Whenever I went to her house, she was at home, and she told me she had been at home all week.

Every time I went to visit her, she was reading a book from the piles that were stacked all around the house. She was reading them all at once, she said. They were broad, on wide topics; she had books on physics and Mayan astrology; she read the Popol Vuh and the Torah and the Quran. She read books on philosophy and on Zen. She told me she was trying to meditate. I was impressed. I asked her how it was going.

'Not very well, I'm afraid. I'm too crazy to meditate. My mind is too crazy.'

'Well, I think it's great. Keep trying.'

'I will. I am.'

'I know.'

On Saturdays, I went to Carmen's house before lunch and Carmen made us food. After lunch we went out for a walk along the shore of the lake. We didn't swim and we didn't go very far. She was unsteady on her feet. She was pale and always cold. She wore a big jumper that she had taken from Dwain, and the same old pair of jeans.

When it got late and I needed to leave, Carmen walked with me back to the pier. I felt sad to leave her alone like this. She did not become sad like me; she was sad but she was sad all the time, and her sadness did not go up or down at any point during the day. Her sadness came out like an acceptance of it all from someone who was too tired to fight. She was sad when I left, she would be sad if I stayed, she had been quietly sad all through the day. Nothing I could do would help. Still, I visited her every Saturday.

When the boat pulled away, Carmen stood at the shore and became smaller and smaller as we moved across the lake. I sat in the back of the boat and turned around to face her. She stood on the shore, watching me leave. When I couldn't see her anymore, I turned and faced ahead. I held it all in until I got back home. I opened the wooden door to my hut and sat on the bed and cried for the rest of the night. Then it got cold and I brushed my teeth and then I went to bed.

I tried to keep in touch with Dwain. I felt I was responsible for Carmen's wellbeing, and I was nervous. I didn't feel qualified. Sometimes I felt that Dwain had run away and I felt angry with him. Other times, I felt sorry for him and I was glad that he was over there. A few weeks turned into two months. He was in San Diego. He never told me what he was doing there.

He sometimes asked how Carmen was and I gave him reports. But I knew he didn't know what to do. I wondered if that was why he had left so soon after Carmen got ill. Because he didn't know how to look after her. I didn't know either but I knew that Carmen and everyone would expect less from me than they would from Dwain. Dwain was like her brother here. I was just her new foreign friend.

So for months, I visited Carmen every week, regardless of whether I wanted to. I visited her when it was hot and when it rained. Every week she was waiting for me at her house, every week she had bought food from the market to cook, and every week when I left her and arrived back at my hut, I sat on the bed and cried.

One week I went to see her and she was excited. She had been at the bookstore that sold books on Mayan linguistics and sociology and anthropology. The academic that Carmen used to talk about was coming to Panajachel. She was giving a talk at the bookshop. Carmen sat in her chair with her knees pressed to her chest. Her hair was loose and dull. She asked me if I would go with her. It was on next Friday night. She seemed timid, almost frightened to go.

'I'll come. That sounds great,' I said.

The following Friday I finished school and walked to the lake and caught the boat. I went straight to Carmen's house. She was ready for the night. She was wearing all navy: navy-blue pants and a navy corduroy shirt. The shirt was long and hung over her pants and made her seem very short. She had brushed her hair. It looked like she had ironed her clothes.

I asked her if she would like to go out to eat, that it would be a treat, for a special occasion. She was pleased. We went to the restaurant on Santander that Carmen had taken me to when I had first got the job. It had brick walls and a fireplace and low ceilings, and each room was divided by an arch. Carmen ordered pasta and drank water. I ordered wine and Carmen looked uncomfortable. I only drank half of it. She kept glancing at the clock. 'I don't want to be late,' she said.

We got to the bookshop early and Carmen wanted to sit up the back, to one side. People stood around holding glasses and talking in low voices. Nobody was sitting yet, but we sat. Carmen was quiet and she watched the academic at the front fiddling with her computer and the projector. The bookshop was small with about twenty seats and when the talk began, all the seats were taken. A few people stood off to the side. In the audience there were older intellectuals, Mayan women who looked like they ran NGOs. There were a few foreigners, but not the touristy type, the sort that were working here as volunteers, or with universities, like Emilie. And there were some Guatemalans in Western clothes who looked like they came from the city.

I watched Carmen watch them all. She was so different from every one of them.

'Look, Ruth, look at all the people here. I wonder who they work for. I wonder if I should talk to them.' But she didn't talk to them and after the presentation was over we hung around and drank tea while Carmen watched the academic. When I asked Carmen if she wanted to talk to her, she laughed and she said no. But she bit her lip and watched other people speak to her or buy her books and get them signed.

'Let's go,' Carmen said. We walked home. The night was cold. Carmen didn't say very much and I thought she was annoyed the way she used to be when I had said the wrong thing. We got to her front door and I waited for her to get the key and let us inside. She stopped and she turned to me without searching for the key. 'Ruth, I'm glad we went to that thing tonight. I'm glad I got to hear her speak.'

She looked in her bag and pulled out the key and unlocked the door and we went inside. She locked the door behind us and it made a clang and she didn't turn on the lights.

She grabbed my arm. 'Ruth, I really think I could be one of them. Those people at the bookshop, academics, or the students. I could be like them, I know I could.'

I squeezed her arm back and we walked down the dark hall and when we got to the kitchen, Carmen turned on the lights.

I stayed at Carmen's that night and in the morning we called Dwain and put him on speaker phone and the three of us were together again. Carmen told Dwain about the talk. I could feel that if Dwain were here, he would look at me.

'Carmen, that's great. It's great that you went.'

'Yeah,' Carmen said softly. 'I'm glad Ruth came. I wanted to talk to the professor afterwards but I was too shy, wasn't I, Ruth?'

'It doesn't matter. You'll get another chance for sure.'

We were all very happy for Carmen.

'I'm actually thinking about doing her course. She runs one each year, in the city I think. Or maybe even try to study with her. She teaches at a university in Texas.'

'Texas – where your uncle lives? It's a good idea, Carmen.'

'Yeah. I'm just thinking about it.' Her cheeks were pale pink. It was a warm day. We were sitting on the steps of Carmen's back patio.

'Hey, I've got to go here. I'm glad you called. Last night sounded great.'

'We miss you, Dwain,' Carmen said. 'Come back soon.'

'I will.'

We hung up the phone and Carmen gave me a squeeze. She was smiling and she didn't say anything. The sun was shining right on us now, and Carmen took off the big beige jumper that she wore all the time these days. She held her arms out to the sun. He skin was so pale you could see her veins. She closed her eyes. I tried to relax. She would be fine now. I looked at her. She would be fine.

18

DURING THE WEEK, I LIVED clean and quietly. I was doing it for Carmen, as if somehow by making myself stable, I could help her, help her life and her recovery. At first I had wanted to change my life for Emilie. Then I wanted to change it for myself. Now I was doing it for Carmen, completely.

I went to bed early, for Carmen, and when I woke, I walked to the lake and back again, walking hard and fast. I worked hard at the school. I was serious. When I came home, I ate a simple meal, and then I carved. To have fun would have felt like a betrayal to her. Fun was not what I was doing anymore.

Carmen didn't ask for this and I didn't tell her about it. I still sometimes spoke to Emilie, we had a lot to talk about now: our work, our lives as expats, two people with their own work to do. Even my conversations with Emilie were for Carmen now, in a way. They were part of my sober life and they helped me to stay healthy and grounded and strong, like eating apples and yoghurt and cabbages. But I didn't tell Emilie any of this either, and I didn't tell Carmen about our calls. I just lived this way, in the background, staying as stable as I could. Carmen didn't have anyone else. She needed me. I even wondered if I should move back to Panajachel, but I decided that my life was just right like this. I didn't want to disrupt the equilibrium.

One week I went to see Carmen at her house and she looked tired and happy. She told me that the academic was running a course in the city for two weeks, and that she had enrolled to do it. It started in one month.

'Oh god, Ruth. I'm so relieved. I've finally found something I actually want to do.'

She made us green tea and we sat on the patio with bare feet. She had stewed the tea for too long and it was bitter. I drank it anyway.

Dwain came back to the lake for two weeks. I didn't see much of him. I heard about his visit from Carmen. He spent time in Panajachel, but he and Carmen did not go out. Carmen told me that he was drinking more than before, and now that she was not drinking at all, things were different between them. I still visited Carmen on Saturdays and we made plans to see Dwain that weekend.

We met Dwain for breakfast. It was his last weekend before he left again. He showed up straight from wherever he had stayed. He was hungover and his hands shook. He ordered a coffee and drank it quickly; he ordered another one straight away. I watched him and I felt sad. Carmen did not notice any of this. She was calm as a rock and she watched the people in the street as though she had never seen tourists before.

After breakfast Dwain and I caught the boat to Jaibalito. Carmen didn't seem to mind. She had a lot of reading to do, she said. She needed us less now than she used to. She wanted to go home and be alone. On the boat, Dwain tried to make small talk and he tried to laugh, but there was distance between him and me. His laughter was sharp and I didn't believe him. I told him about Carmen, about her plans, about how well she seemed.

'Yeah, it's great,' he said, but he was staring at his hands.

The boat docked and we walked together up the hill. I didn't want to leave it like this. I turned to face him. I squinted. The sun was setting behind his back. I could smell him, a mixture of sweat and alcohol and something else, something familiar to me.

'Dwain, come back. Come back and live here. This is where you belong. You were born here, you grew up here. What are you trying to do over there?'

He didn't look at me. He wasn't surprised. He sighed.

'Ruth, you don't get it. Carmen is right. You're not from here.' He waited, as though wondering if he should speak. 'Don't you get it by now? There's no future here. Carmen's right about this place. It sucks you in and if you stay, it drives you crazy. It won't let you leave. This place always wins.'

'That's not true. Look at Carmen. Look at how well she is now. And she stayed.'

Dwain looked at me now for the first time that day; he glanced at me briefly and then he looked over the lake.

'She's doing well. Yep. How long have you lived here, Ruth?'

'Two years now.'

'Two years. Right. Right.' He was being gentle, but there was an edge to him now that I hadn't seen before. He was trying to save his life. And he didn't have any idea how. I had thought I knew things, but now I saw that I had no idea what Dwain was going through.

Dwain left, and a week after that, Carmen left for the city for her course. For the first week that Carmen was there, she sent me messages telling me about the course. She had arranged to stay in the student rooms attached to the university. She sent me photos of her room and of the courtyard garden and the roses she could see from her room. She sent me a photo of the books for her course, laid out neatly on the desk, with the plastic bag from the bookshop spread out flat next to it. She sent me a photo she had taken sneakily of the academic standing in her woven dress. Then I didn't hear from her again and I assumed she was busy with the course. After the two weeks were up, I texted her to see when she was coming back. She didn't reply. I waited two days and then I messaged again. When I hadn't heard from her for two more days, I messaged Dwain.

'Onto it. I'm in touch with her family. I'll let you know.'

I didn't hear anything for one week. Then Dwain texted and told me they had found her in a house in the city and her uncle was coming to look after her.

I didn't see Carmen for a month after that. I heard from Dwain that she was in the city hospital but when I asked about going to visit her, he told me that she was in a different hospital and she was only allowed visits from family. It sounded like prison.

Emilie called me one day after work. I told her about Carmen.

'That's terrible. Is she okay?'

I told her that I thought she was but that I had not seen her yet. It was the second time this had happened to her. And this time it seemed worse.

Emilie didn't get it though, and she moved on to other things. She asked about my work and Jaibalito as if those things still mattered now. Dwain had left, Carmen was in hospital. And Emilie didn't seem to get it at all. I wanted to get off the phone.

Carmen sent me a message on Monday afternoon.

'I'm out! I'm coming back home. I'll be back in Pana on Wednesday.'

I couldn't go and see her on Wednesday because of my work at the school. On Friday afternoon when I finished my last class, I went straight to catch a boat. I didn't even go home.

Carmen opened the door before I knocked; she was breathless and she smelled of clean clothes. I hugged her and she hugged me back and she felt tiny against my body.

Carmen took me through to the living room. There was a blanket on the couch as though she had been lying there when I arrived. She ate grapes from a brown paper bag that was so worn it looked like fabric. Her uncle was sitting in the armchair, reading a newspaper. He looked tired. He smiled at me when I came in, and the smiling made him seem even more tired.

We sat outside, in the garden, on the deck, our feet dangling in the air. Carmen seemed like a lake, still, with little breeze.

'No, but this was a bad one, Ruth.' Carmen looked at me and smiled and put her head on my shoulder. 'My little Ruth. No, it was bad. My uncle had to come out. He stayed near the hospital and he came to visit me every single day that I was there. And he's still here, staying for another week, he thinks.' Carmen gazed out over the garden. 'It's actually kind of nice having someone to live with. Even if it is my uncle. Even if he is only here because I'm crazy.'

'You're not crazy, Carmen.'

'It is nice though. Especially at night. It's so dark here, you know? I never realised that before. It's so dark here at night that you can wake up and not know if you are alive or dead. It's nice then to hear my uncle breathing in the next room. I think I've been alone for too long. I can't really help it though. That's just how my life is.'

'Where's Dwain? Did he come and visit you too?'

'Dwain?' Carmen looked confused. 'I don't know. The States. He's probably on a Greyhound bus chatting up some girl.' Carmen let out a tired laugh. She put her arm around me. 'And you, little Ruthita? Got your life sorted out yet? Surely you have married Emilie by now. Or has she gone and married someone else?'

I ignored the last thing she said. 'I'm fine. Normal, you know. I mean, not normal but living normally. Just working. I'm boring. But fine, you know.'

'Fine. Fine. What does "fine" even mean anymore.' She said this more to herself than to me, quietly, her voice floating into the afternoon air.

'What do you think you will do, Carmen?'

‘Oh, I don’t know. I need to do something different, don’t I? That much is obvious. Even I can see that. My uncle is trying to help me figure that out. Maybe I’ll move to the States. Pretend I’m from there and not from here for a while. Fuck. Imagine living there, all superhighways and McDonald’s stores. But maybe that would be good for me. Maybe too much beauty is bad for the nerves, the way that too much fun can be.’

She raised an arm and waved it around her head and smiled sweetly. ‘Paradise hasn’t exactly worked out for me. Maybe ugliness and neurotic people is what I need after all.’

From time to time, the uncle, who was reading inside, peered at us over his glasses. He looked at Carmen, then at me, then at Carmen again. He looked at her like she was a puzzle that he couldn’t figure out how to solve.

19

Carmen went to America, in the end. She lived with her aunt and uncle in Texas. 'Just for a while,' she told me on the phone. 'He wouldn't leave without me and he wanted to go home. It was just easier to come back with him. I'm living with them. Can you imagine, thirty-three and living in the spare room of your uncle and aunt's. Their kids are all grown up so they have loads of room. I think they need a project now that they're empty nesters. The town is okay.'

'What do you do there all day?'

'What do I do? Oh, I don't even know. I walk around a lot. All day, some days. At first it made my aunt crazy, she freaked out, but now she's chilled out a bit and the only rule she has is that I have to be back by dark. Like a teenager.'

'You don't get bored?'

'Nah. What's there to be bored about? I'm just trying to stay alive. That's all I've ever done, really. At least now I'm honest about it, and not pretending anymore. Not pretending to be cool.'

'I'm glad you're alive, Carmen.'

'Me too, Ruth.'

I was happy for Carmen when she moved to America, and I was also relieved. She would be okay now. I made sure I was too busy or too tired to think. I was tired all the time these days. I didn't dream anymore. I was still in love with the lake, but I loved it now in a practical way.

I didn't hear from Emilie much anymore, and I didn't call her either. At first, when we were still talking from time to time, I went to send her a message, but I didn't, or I wrote one but deleted it, or I walked to the lake with the intention of calling her but just sat on the jetty instead. I didn't know why I did all those things, or why it was so hard to stay in contact with her. I wondered if she did the same thing with me. No, I decided, probably not. She was too practical to write a message that she wouldn't send. She just wouldn't write one at all. I imagined her getting on with her life, busy and far away in a city with lights. I imagined her at work, feeling fulfilled and hanging out with her friends on Friday night. Emilie didn't need me anymore and that was something I understood. I didn't blame her. I was sort of the same.

It wasn't that I didn't need Emilie, but that my problems felt too big to solve. They got in the way. I didn't want to lie to her and I didn't want to tell her the truth. It was easier not to talk to her at all than to tell her what I was going through.

And what was I going though? The feeling of blankness had returned. The feeling that everything around me was fake. Feeling like this was worse than feeling sad. At least with grief, you feel alive. I had felt alive when I was with Carmen and Dwain. I had thought the feeling was my own and that it was mine to keep. It was only now that they had gone away and the emptiness had come back again that I realised the progress I thought I had made had just been pretending and filling in time.

I didn't talk to anyone now, not Emilie or Carmen or Dwain. I did my job at the school during the day, and at nights I carved. I lived like a functional household piece. I did the job at the school that I was assigned to do and I didn't care, or feel anything. Life was not supposed to be like this. And yet this is how my life was.

Sometimes, on my very low days, I thought of Carmen and remembered her here at the lake with afternoon sun in her hair, rolling her eyes, calling us tourists. When I thought of Dwain I felt sad but then I remembered Carmen and I was filled with hope, for her and for all of us. About Emilie, I didn't feel joy or despair. She had never been lost and she didn't need help, from me or anybody else.

I lived how I imagined other people lived. I got up early and walked before work. I spent all day at the school. I ate lunch with the teachers and we spoke of small things. I went home and made dinner and, while there was light, I made figurines.

I had started burning them though, instead of throwing them into the lake. I didn't know why I burnt each one, except that it felt good to make something and then watch it burn, and it felt good to feel good for a moment. For a moment my eyes were locked on the shape of the flame and I did not think and that was what I wanted the most. Not to think was such a relief.

Carmen started writing me letters by hand. I could tell her mood from her handwriting. She had enrolled in classes at a community college. She was trying to get enough credit to enter university. She still wanted to go to university to study anthropology. She wrote about it in her letters.

'And then I could come back to Guate and work there. I might need to move to Antigua, or even the city. I don't know how much work there is at the lake for an anthropologist. There might be though. I just don't know.'

In the summer Carmen wrote to me again. 'I've done it! I got in! I'm going to university! I got into a program in San Antonio at the university where the professor works. She teaches there and I can take one of her courses in second and third year. Wish me luck, Ruthie. I'm so nervous.' And then, a few weeks later she wrote, 'I'm here! I start school next week. I'm living above a Mexican restaurant. All my clothes smell like beans. It's one room and I sleep and eat in the same room. Well. It's cheap and my uncle is paying and it's all he can afford. I'm even going to do the work program here. Working and studying at the same time – can you believe it? I might not have any time to write anymore. I don't know how I'll cope. There must be another me inside this one that can do it all.'

I didn't hear from Carmen after that. I missed her, but I knew she was busy with school, and I was happy for her. I knew she had her family, and they were looking after her. Two months went by. I continued with my life. The next time I heard about Carmen was from Dwain. He came and he told me that Carmen was dead.

20

THE NIGHT BEFORE I HEARD about Carmen, I saw her in a dream. She was in a boat in Türkiye; it was moving very fast. She wore all black and she looked glamorous, and she was older too. She was going along the river, heading somewhere fast. She was happy and she had business to do.

It was Dwain who told me. He came to my place one day. I was outside on the porch and I was surprised to see him walking up the hill. I hadn't known he was back from America. Then I saw the way that he walked and how he looked and I knew it wasn't good. He walked slowly, with his head down, and by the time he got to me, I knew for sure what he had come here to say.

I tried to put it off. I made us both coffee, which I prepared outside, on my little gas stove. It was midday and I had just gotten back home after a walk. I search through my food basket to see what I had to eat. I held out a can of beans. 'You hungry?' I said.

'Ruth, I have to tell you something. It's not good.'

I put down the beans. 'Don't say it. I know. When did you hear?'

'Last night. I was already here. I got here yesterday afternoon.'

'I had a dream.'

'Me too.'

As soon as Dwain started telling me, I wanted him to stop. I knew what he was telling me and I wasn't ready yet. I felt panicky, like I had forgotten to do something important. I wanted to brush my teeth, I wanted to clean my room, I wanted to go down to the lake and sit and get my mind straight before he said what he was going to say. But here he was, talking anyway, and there was nothing I could do about it. Once he said them, his words would not go away.

Carmen had disappeared, he said, for a few days, like she used to do. Her uncle and aunt were not used to it, though, and her aunt panicked and called the police. The first night her uncle and aunt didn't sleep. They both stayed up all night. They searched for days. The police said they couldn't do very much except alert her friends and wait. Carmen didn't have any friends. Her uncle and aunt didn't know who to call. They drove around the neighbourhood like they were looking for a teenage girl.

On the fourth day, the police called. Some kids from a squat in the city had told them that a girl there had passed out. They said they didn't know who she was. They didn't know on what day she passed out, and they didn't know that she was dead.

Her uncle and aunt had to go to the morgue and confirm that it was her. Carmen had looked more alive than dead, her aunt had told Dwain. That almost made me smile though I didn't know why. *So, she is dead*, I thought. It didn't seem real. I tried saying it to myself again and I must have said it out loud this time because Dwain looked at me and he said, 'Yes'.

'So, what's next?' I didn't even know what I meant. I felt like half a person, like a person cut in half, missing something important.

'Well,' Dwain said. 'There'll be the funeral. I don't know if you'll want to go. It should be held here. But it will be held in the States. So that her parents and her family can go.'

I tried to say 'right' but no words came and I just nodded and then started to cry. So that was it, I thought. I wouldn't even get to say goodbye.

'I'm hoping they can bring some of her ashes here. I think she did actually love it here, despite everything, you know.' I nodded, still crying. 'Ruth—'

'Don't.' I didn't even know what he was going to say. I didn't want him to say anything. There was nothing he could say that would fix any of this. I was suddenly furious at him. He had left. He had not been here at all. Why was he here now? He could have just called. He was pretending to be part of my life when he wasn't part of it anymore. He had left this place, he had left me, and he had left Carmen too.

He tried to keep talking and I didn't respond. When he left, he told me he was here for a week and that we should see each other again. He stood in front of me, looking guilty. I felt bad for him but the bad feeling couldn't reach up through the layers of grief. I wanted him gone.

He left and it was quiet. I sat without moving all afternoon. When it got dark, I stood up and I took two steps through my door and I went to bed. I didn't even get changed. As I waited to fall asleep, I realised I had known all along. I had known this would happen and I had tried to prevent it, thinking that I could stop things like this. Now, it was done. I couldn't fight anymore. I fell asleep, and when I woke, it was dawn.

I saw Dwain again the next day. He came in the morning, with his dirty hair and slow walk, and for a moment I felt that I had dreamt yesterday up, and now it was happening all over again but in real life this time. But instead of telling me that Carmen had died, he sat on the log, not saying anything. I made coffee like I did yesterday. I handed him the cup. He tried to smile. I tried to smile back.

We sat in silence for a long time. I moved my toes around in the dirt and I watched them slowly go brown. I felt wild. An avocado landed with a thump to my right. I tried to make a mental note to go and pick it up later but the note wouldn't stick in my mind.

We held our cups but we didn't drink. Our coffee had gone cold when I offered Dwain another. He looked at the cup he held in his hand and seemed surprised, and then took a sip.

'You know, I always thought she seemed more like a ghost than a living person,' I said, not knowing why.

Dwain seemed annoyed. He shook his head. 'Come on, Ruth. What are you talking about?'

We were silent again for another long pause. I stared out over the water, which I could see in patches through the trees. I wished Dwain wasn't here. I wished he had never come. Why had he not been a better friend? I wanted to be alone.

I broke the silence without looking up. 'What do you think you'll do?'

'What do you mean? Stay here, I guess. Oh, right. Without her. I don't know.' Dwain paused, as if thinking. 'I don't know,' he said again. He pushed his hair off his face. His head hung low. He had a patch of pimples on his chin. 'She tried, you know? She tried, and it killed her. It makes me think that it's not worth trying at all. That it's the trying that will kill you. The wanting other things. You can't escape your life. That's just how it is. It's dangerous to want other things.' He raised his head and he looked at me, then past me, over my shoulder, to my neighbour's place.

He poked at the ground with a stick. Dirt flew up and hit the bottom of his jeans and landed on the top of his foot. He tossed the stick away. He turned to me. His eyes were suddenly empty and feral. It was like he was missing something fundamental.

'What are you going to do, Ruth?'

'What do you mean?'

'You can't live here forever, you know. You're not from here. You should get out. Go home.'

I laughed but it was more like a puff of air, or a snort. 'Home. Right. That's what Emilie says too. That I can't stay here forever.'

He was quiet. Then he breathed in. 'You know what? Do what you want. Whatever works for you. Just do whatever works, Ruth.' He kicked at the dirt and then he stood up. He looked down at me, his face contorted in pain. 'Don't be a stranger, Ruth. Come and visit sometime.'

I said I would, and then Dwain left.

—

I spoke to Emilie the next day.

'Fuck, Ruth. Shit. I'm sorry. I don't know what to say. What are you going to do?'

'Why does everyone keep asking me that? What does this change? About anything?' I could smell the sea. I smelled incense. I could hear other things, things that weren't here at the lake. The world seemed even more baffling than it did before. 'I'm going to stay, of course. What does this change? It doesn't change anything.'

A speedboat roared past in the distance, in the direction of Panajachel. After a minute I heard ripples from the boat land on the shore. They were longer and slower than the normal waves.

'I'm going to stay,' I said.

'Okay. I got it, Ruth.'

'Emilie. I'm going to stay.'

One night she came to me. She came to me in a dream but the dream felt real. She could not speak but she looked very calm. She sort of floated and she waved at me. I tried to call out but I could not speak. She smiled and then she floated away, and then she was gone. I woke up saying my own name.

I didn't take any time off from school. Nothing had changed anyway. Things were the way that they had been for those months when Carmen was in America. It was the same as that, except permanent.

I relied on routines because I was a shell. I was an empty body just walking around. My routines were the only thing holding me up and as long as I had them, I looked like a person. But there was nothing inside me. I kept the same schedule of classes at school and no-one knew what had happened. I told no-one about Carmen because nobody cared. They had heard rumours but no-one knew what to believe, and in the end, they didn't care. They all thought Carmen was a junkie anyway. I kept to my regular school routine, but I was pretending, and in the evenings I had no energy left. I didn't carve anymore, I didn't do anything. I didn't go down to the lake. I stayed in my hut and I stared at the wall. I didn't even sit outside.

On weekends I did the same, and sometimes I tried to walk fast up the hill. I found I couldn't walk fast anymore. I walked up the hill very slowly, and when I got to the top I stayed for an hour or two. Up there was the only place I found something like peace. There were no people. There weren't even trees. There was only the silence and the breeze. The silence was thick and with the lake so far below, I felt that my own life was far away too, which felt good. I went up there every chance I could.

At first, I wanted to talk to Dwain. I called him, I messaged him; he didn't respond. I thought he would call back, that we would talk, that we would become family now that Carmen was gone. But he didn't call and he didn't text back and after a while I stopped waiting for him. I walked past his house and the shutters were closed. Dwain was not coming back.

Emilie had started calling me, though. I ignored her calls. I didn't want to pretend to be fine the way I had to pretend to be fine at school. I had no energy for that. She called a lot and when I didn't respond, she sent me a message saying that she had called, and that she hoped I was doing alright. Then she sent just a question mark.

Things became tighter around me. My life became small. All the pretending, all the staring at walls. I did not know how to get through this time. I knew I needed to do something. But I didn't know what to do.

One Saturday I couldn't get up. I could hear the neighbour chopping wood and his children playing in the yard. Sometimes they played in mine. I couldn't get up and do my usual walk, and I cursed myself; I needed routines. I tried to get up but I couldn't move. I stayed in bed the whole day.

On Sunday it was the same, and I felt unclean, like a dirty windscreen, and wrong, as though I shouldn't be alive. I had the feeling of floating in space, untethered, in the dark. I couldn't find my way back to earth, back to light and warmth and growing things. I was beyond any force that could pull me back in.

On Monday I went to the school and I was relieved and I pretended, and the pretending even worked for a bit, at least while I was there. I vowed to pretend even more after that. I vowed to pretend even to myself and that next weekend I would walk up the hill, no matter how I felt or did not feel. When I got home, I couldn't move again, but that didn't matter. I stared at the wall; staring at the wall had become part of my routine.

The following weekend I forced myself up the hill. It was hard. I had to stop and take rests. I sat there all day. It was cold and wet and I did not want to be there. But I had nowhere that I wanted to be. I was stuck. Carmen had died. She was dead. I couldn't believe it. I hated her. I hated Dwain. I didn't even want to cry. They had gone. I had thought it was real – their friendship, and them. But now they were both gone.

I walked slowly back down the hill, but the side of the hill was wet, and on the way down, I slipped. I was covered with mud all down one side, and my face and my hands were muddy too. I got to my hut, wet and muddy, barely feeling human at all. There was a basket of food from the shop on the porch. And next to the basket was Emilie, sitting on my wooden stool.

21

EMILIE WAS EATING A MUESLI bar, and when she saw me, she stopped eating and stood up. Her large body was awkward. She shifted to one side. She waved hello in an awkward way. She smiled nervously.

I walked straight to her and, without saying hello, I fell on her and held her in a hug. She felt like a hot bath. I held her and I felt her pull away, but I held on and leant my weight on her. She relaxed; she had understood, she would not pull away now. I cried old and stale tears. Dry, hard sobs came out in small chunks. When I was done, I didn't look at her. I was ashamed of what I had become. I was wet and covered with mud and dirt. I knew I looked awful and I felt how I looked. I knew I could not pretend with her. Not now that she was here, just standing there.

Emilie watched me and didn't say anything. She went into the hut ahead of me and she stopped and looked around. She took my bag down from the shelf and she started packing things. She made the bed and looked around again and then she pushed me out. She turned to me and spoke for the first time since she arrived.

'Come on. We're going to Panajachel.'

Emilie had rented a room with two beds and she brought me to stay with her. I had a hot shower until the hot water ran out and when I came out Emilie had laid some food on one of the beds. 'Eat,' she said. Apart from that, she didn't talk to me.

We went for a walk along the lake and when we got back to the room, I went to bed. Emilie sat up and read. I fell asleep and when I woke up it was midnight and Emilie was still awake and reading on top of the covers of her bed. She looked at me and didn't say anything and I loved her then, even more than before.

We did the same thing, every day. Every day, Emilie instructed me. She showed me how to live and what to do, and it was the basic things. Hot showers, food, very slow walks. And lots of time for sleep.

After two weeks, we went back to Jaibalito. I felt the faintest flicker of life inside. Emilie cleaned my hut and opened the windows and the door. She sorted out the area where I stored all the food. She had conversations with the neighbours that she didn't tell me about. She washed and changed the sheets and she hung the wet sheets out to dry. I didn't know if I still had a job but Emilie told me not to worry about it. She said it was fine. She told me that she had spoken to Miguel and he understood and he was taking care of it. She told me he said that they were fine at the school and I only needed to return when I felt ready and strong.

Emilie had to go back to Pátzcuaro, to go back to work. She could only take two weeks off, she said. She said that she felt bad about it, and she kept asking me if I would be okay with a twisted expression on her face. I told her that I would be fine and I kept saying it to make her feel okay. When she left, she gave me a concerned look, and she told me to call her every day. I said that I would, and that I would be fine, and then she was gone again.

When Emilie left, my life had changed, in a different way to how it changed when we first met. Emilie had come, solid as wood, and she had re-arranged things. Now, at last, I could feel my grief, and it felt like flowing water.

I cried now instead of staring at the wall. I was crying for Carmen, but for more than that, too – I was crying for what my life had become and for what it had been before Carmen as well; I was crying for the things I had looked for and that I had not found. I cried so hard that I vomited. I was emptying myself out, and that felt good, though I never stayed empty for long. After I had cried, I slept heavily; when I woke up, the feelings began to build up once more and the whole cycle started again. I was a process and not a person at all.

Dwain told me, in an email, that some of Carmen's ashes were being buried in Jaibalito. They would be buried up there, high on the hill, next to the large white cross that I had seen when I was swimming in the water that day, long ago, when I had first moved to the lake. I didn't go to the ceremony. I didn't visit her grave afterwards. I didn't know what I would say to her. Instead, I walked around and past Dwain's house and when the memories of that place rose in me, I pushed them back down and kept on walking.

One afternoon, I ran into Miguel. He stepped into my path as I came near Dwain's house as though he had been expecting me. He greeted me, then he invited me to his house to have a coffee. Without waiting for an answer, he said to follow him and he turned around and started walking. I followed him the way a child would, too tired to protest, and when I got to his house his wife took both her hands and placed them on mine; she looked into my eyes and didn't say anything but nodded and smiled in a very small way that showed she pitied me. I could feel her rough and callused skin. Then she motioned to two wooden stools in the dirt outside the front door. She moved around the kitchen and Miguel and I stayed outside and sat on the stools.

Miguel hung his head and rested his elbows on his knees so that the weight of his body brought him all the way forwards. He didn't talk at all until his wife brought the coffee, and then, before he had his first sip, he asked me if I didn't want to visit Carmen's grave. No, I said. But I said it too quickly; Miguel raised his head and looked at me. He asked me what I was doing about work. Nothing, I said. I told him I was taking time off from the school. What was I planning to do? I didn't know, I said, too tired to pretend to be cheerful or to have any plans. Miguel sipped and looked towards the hills. I could see the creases beside his eyes.

'You should go back to the school,' he said. He nodded. 'You should go back and finish your job.' He spoke for a few minutes, telling me why, telling me what to do. He said the same thing over and over again in lots of different ways. He had only one message for me: that it was time to return to my life.

I didn't understand why he was telling me all this. We spoke some more, about mundane things; mainly Miguel asked me questions and sat quietly, listening. But when I went back home, I thought about what he said, about work, about my life. I imagined returning to the school. Just imagining it felt like hard work. But imagining it was changing something.

On Monday one week after that, I went back to the school. I could see from the expression on the teachers' faces that they were not expecting me, that they were confused, but also that they didn't really care. The air was warm and the windows were open. The sand on the soccer field looked new. I could smell spring. I smelled varnish. I went to see the principal and I started to explain. He cut me off.

'Don Miguel has told us everything. Don't worry, Ruth. We have arranged everything. Come back when you are ready.'

I told him that I was ready right now and he looked at me briefly, then said that was fine. He would let the other teachers know, and I could come back tomorrow, if I liked. For the rest of the day, I cleaned out my hut. I pulled the furniture outside and my belongings too and I dusted everything. The neighbour came out of her house holding a basket of laundry. She glanced at me curiously over the fence and then she moved on. I swept the floor and moved everything back but I arranged it differently from before. Instead of being in the centre of the room, I put the bed against the back wall. I kept the kitchen plank where it was along the side. Now there was an open space in the middle of the room where I could sit and even put my wooden stool. I got my clothes out ready for the next day. I lay on my bed and tested it out. From my bed now I could see the whole room, the kitchen area, the window, and the door. It was fine, I decided. It could even be good.

22

THOUGH I DIDN'T FEEL LIKE talking, Emilie called me a lot. She called and she chatted to me about the most mundane things. I listened to her like the radio. She didn't seem to mind though. She had called me one day and just talked to me like this. Then she had called again the next day.

I heard only snippets and I realised that she was sending me postcards from the living world. *Scrambled eggs for dinner, I spilled some jam, the neighbour's dog chased a chicken.* She talked about the people she worked with and one who had just gotten married and how, now that the wedding was over, she was depressed and baked cakes every weekend and she brought them into work. Everyone in the office was getting fat. She talked about how the council had started cleaning the streets outside her office in the afternoons. She couldn't hear anything if she had a video call. She told me about anything. She painted a world for me that I wasn't part of. As though I was a hospital patient, confined to bed, and she was the nurse talking about the weather outside. Every day, she did this and at first I tolerated the calls and then I relaxed and then I even started enjoying them. She was giving this to me, these conversations. She was not asking for anything.

Without Dwain, without Carmen, my life was small. Whenever I felt strong emotions coming on, I narrowed myself down to the width I needed to be to feel steady again. On the really bad days, I narrowed myself so much that I was just the exact moment I was in. To think beyond that moment, either forwards or behind, would bring on such anxiety that I couldn't go to school; I couldn't be around anyone. I couldn't do anything except go back to bed, and that was the thing I was trying to avoid most of all. I narrowed myself.

With Carmen gone, I noticed Emilie more. For Carmen, Emilie was never interesting enough. She was too predictable. There were no wild moods and you could never be sure that Emilie would really say what she thought. But I didn't have to keep up with Carmen anymore. Emilie was predictable, and predictable was good.

Emilie asked me to come and visit her. I didn't say no but I didn't say anything, and I didn't do anything about it. One day, she said she was coming back to visit me. For what, I thought. But I was happy too.

In the days before Emilie arrived, I cleaned up my hut as best as I could. It didn't take long and it still didn't look very clean. There was the dirt floor, the mudbrick walls and the wooden windows with shutters but no glass. But I tidied my things and to me it looked nice. I watched the sun go down. I had the strange feeling that something would change. That this was one of the last times I would be on my own. I didn't take the feeling seriously, though. I had been wrong about that kind of thing before.

When Emilie arrived, she looked around at the hut, with everything so clean and neat, and she raised an eyebrow.

'Nice,' she said, and I couldn't tell what she meant. I had been nervous of her visit, in spite of myself. It wasn't until she sat down on the stool and I brought her coffee and I sat down in the dirt that I noticed how thin she was. She was drawn. I realised that this whole time I had been thinking about myself, not her. She had been a comfort to me. I had no idea what was going on for her.

Emilie slept next to me in my bed. We talked into the night, and the night was wide. Emilie talked differently when it was night, like she used to in Panajachel. She talked and I listened, pleased to have a job to do.

In the morning, Emilie had gotten up early and started cooking while I was still asleep. She had searched through my pantry stack and had moved the camping stove outside. I got up and wrapped myself in a blanket and sat outside, on the stool. The morning was cold. Emilie stirred the pot, concentrating. Steam billowed around her head. I stared at the road.

'What do you want to do today? Do you want to go somewhere? We could catch the boat to San Marcos or something?'

Emilie didn't look up. 'I'm tired today. Can we just hang out here?'

We stayed in Jaibalito that day and the following day too, and even when I went to work, Emilie stayed at home and wandered around the village. She seemed reluctant to leave, almost as though she was afraid. She had changed. I thought about those first few weeks we had spent together in Panajachel. Emilie had always wanted to be doing something, going somewhere, talking to other foreigners.

Each day we passed in the same way, living quietly during the day and talking for hours in the dark each night. The only thing that changed in those days was how far apart we slept. The first night we slept facing different ways. By the time she left, we fell asleep in an embrace.

Miguel came to see me one day, a few weeks after Emilie left. I was surprised when he came, and a little ashamed. My hut was not set up for guests. I made coffee. He stayed outside, standing politely. I gave Miguel the stool to sit on and I sat on the step. We drank the coffee in silence at first. Miguel commented on different things; there was a lot of space between each thing he said. I had learnt to wait. I waited now.

He looked at the sky. 'It hasn't rained much this month.'

I looked around, then up at the trees. 'No,' I said. 'It's been very dry.'

We were quiet. Miguel took a sip. I did too.

'But it has been cold.'

I moved my feet and didn't say anything. I could smell smoke in the air from the neighbours' fire. It was early afternoon, but it was already cold.

He took a breath and he spoke again without looking at me. 'You have been here for some time, Ruth. Time has gotten away, as they say. I'm surprised that you have stayed with us for so long.'

I felt uneasy. 'Has the school gotten tired of me? Do they want me to leave?'

'The people are happy to have you here. But I think of you. I wonder why you don't leave. After all that has happened here.'

'I don't want to leave.' I said it firmly, staring straight at him.

'I see.' He took a breath, then paused, and nodded at the ground.

I spoke again. 'This is my home. Carmen is here.'

Miguel didn't look at me but he looked past me, through the trees. The sun was low and orange. He spoke gently but with authority. 'This is not your home. You are not from here. Remember who you are.'

I didn't say anything. Remember who I was. Who was I? Tears came to my eyes. I didn't speak anymore. There was nothing left to say. He nodded again, almost privately this time, absorbed in his own thoughts. He stood up. He looked me in the eye for the first time since he arrived and he took a step closer to me.

'You have a duty to accept the trajectory of your life. You must not fight. If you try to fight your life, you will lose.'

He looked at me hard, urging me to see what he saw. He tipped up his cup and drank the last of the coffee, which was cold by now. Then he nodded and he turned and left, walking slowly down the hill. He looked like an old man now, frail and small. When he had been talking to me, he had seemed powerful and big.

I went inside my hut. I heard his footsteps grow faint on the path. And then it was quiet again.

I don't know when I decided to move to Pátzcuaro. I don't even remember telling Emilie. One day I thought it and then it was real and suddenly it was happening.

Emilie was pleased and she disguised it with practicalities. She said I should fly there, that it was the quickest way. I told her I wanted to go by land.

I also wanted to finish the school year. The school was my one link to the world. My job there was my one responsibility. I told the school of my plans. They weren't surprised. I gave away my things and I started saying my goodbyes.

By the end of the school year, I had given everything away except for the things that had come with the hut. The hut looked the same as the day I arrived.

On my last night I sat at the jetty for the very last time. I watched the sun go down. I had even bought a bottle of beer at the shop and I drank it as day became night. I remembered Carmen and Dwain and how we sat here and talked and we had even laughed.

On my way back up the hill it was almost dark, but not quite. I ran into a student from school. I liked her; she was small and she was serious and she took her classes seriously. She worked hard and she was smart and learning quickly. When she saw me, she stopped. Her mother stood behind.

'Miss Ruth, you are leaving. When do you leave? Is it soon? We will miss you when you go.'

'I'll miss you too.'

'I wish you could have seen our chickens. They are so big. One is black, the rest are white.'

'They sound wonderful.'

She looked at me with round sweetness now. 'Will you come back and teach us again soon?'

'I don't know. No. I don't think so. No.'

'Okay. Bye then!' She waved at me in a gesture that was too big for how close she was to me. She walked past and continued down to the lake. The mother followed behind her and she smiled as she passed.

I didn't sleep very much that night. I had to catch the first boat. I woke up often throughout the night, waking into the darkness. I woke again and when I checked the time, it was time to get up and go. It was still dark when I left the hut. I closed the door and put my backpack on and walked down to the boat, feeling my way with my feet.

I didn't look back when the boat left the jetty. I was feeling something and I wanted to remember it. Jaibalito had entered me. Like Carmen, it was no longer a physical thing. It had become a space inside that was real. Like Carmen, it had changed me. Like Carmen, too, it would never leave.

23

THE TRIP FROM THE LAKE to Pátzcuaro was long. I liked travelling through the night. The land outside the window was so dark that you didn't know if you were moving at all. There was just the noise of the tyres on the long straight road, the bumps and the moving from side to side. Then there was morning and the morning light and I had arrived in Mexico.

From Mexico City, I had to catch another, smaller bus, down to Pátzcuaro. After the wide night, the morning felt small. Women loaded baskets onto the bus and when they boarded they smiled at me. The solemnity of Guatemala was gone. Mexico was a new thing.

The bus arrived in Pátzcuaro at ten o'clock in the morning. When I arrived, Emilie was waiting for me, standing on the side of the road. She wore a rumpled linen shirt and her hair stood up like it always did. She looked around. She had not seen me yet. Then she saw me and she smiled wide and then she seemed embarrassed and ran her hand through her hair.

Emilie took my bag and carried it over one shoulder as we walked from the bus stop to her house. She lived on the edge of the centre of town. Inside her house was cooler than outside and it had tiled floors everywhere. Even the living room had tiled floors, over which Emilie had laid a jute mat. The windows were open to the warm Mexican air, and the whole house was olive green and mustard and brown.

Emilie took me to her room and she put my bag in the corner. She showed me the place in her wardrobe where she had cleared some shelves out for me. Then she walked me to the kitchen where she had laid the table with breakfast things. There was bread, jam and an empty mug. Emilie pointed to the coffee pot on the stove. 'I've already put the coffee in.'

I was afraid she would be awkward and talk about things, things about us, like our living together, about what it was exactly we were trying to do. But I ate, and Emilie didn't talk about anything serious. I was relieved and I realised how nervous I had been. I was nervous but she was simple the way she had been when she came to the lake after Carmen had died.

Emilie had to go back to work. After she left, I was in a daze. I made tea and sat in the courtyard in the sun. The concrete was hot under my feet. I moved around the house, looking at Emilie's things. She had simple wooden furniture and a lot of empty space, which made it seem like she had just arrived and wasn't staying long. There was a table in the corner of the living room with small items from her travels and her work. I could see now that she wasn't pretending. She really, actually loved what she did.

—

After the lake, Pátzcuaro felt big. There were cars on the streets and people walked quickly, carrying packages and bags and other things. There were shops that sold wrapped sandwiches. There were gutters in the street and there was a business feeling here that I had not felt for years. There were school buses. And schools, and children in school uniforms who walked around the streets in groups. There were trucks, some large, most of them small, bringing in boxes of vegetables and fruit or plastic-wrapped packages of building materials.

That first Friday night, we went to the expat bar. Emilie lived close by and we walked. The bar was a long and narrow room. Wooden tables lined both walls. Pink and red lights hung from the ceiling. The bar was at the back and there were tables out the front, on the street, where people walked. The whole place had a cosmopolitan air. I felt like I was from the countryside.

There was a large table near the back, filled with a loud group of foreigners, and that was where Emilie walked now. The people at the table were athletic and confident in a European way. I learnt that they worked for different NGOs and had been here for different lengths of time, but most had been here for a few years. They met here every Friday night. Each one of them knew why they were here; they were here with a purpose and their purpose determined what they did with their days. Emilie fit in perfectly.

That night, we sat around the table and everyone talked and drank. Sometimes we talked as one big group; later in the evening there were lots of small groups. People came and went throughout the night; they drank red wine or beer in tall glasses. The women had long and messy hair; the men had stubble and wore Mexican scarves. Many of them stepped out the front to smoke. But they were still serious and at the end of the night they left to go home, focused and clear about their lives.

On the way back home, I asked Emilie about them. She shrugged to each thing that I asked. She barely seemed to know them at all. I said this to her; she shrugged again.

'What do you want me to say? They are my friends. I don't go to bed with them. I don't know what they have for breakfast, or if they snore.' I stopped asking about them.

Emilie noticed different things and she pointed them out. 'Look at that sign – and the garage door! The building above – that's really old.' She was fascinated by the place she was in. She was born to be a sociologist. It was almost like she didn't have any thoughts at all; there was just the physical place that she was in and the way that she interacted with it.

I thought about the lake, and about Carmen and Dwain. It all felt very far away, as though it had happened to someone else who had written about it in a book, which I had read. We crossed the empty plaza. The streetlights made an orange glow. Someone we couldn't see shouted and then laughed. The sound bounced around the heavy walls.

In those first months in Pátzcuaro, I felt so changed that sometimes in the middle of the night I woke up and I couldn't remember my name. For thirty seconds or sometimes more, I lay there, in the dark, trying to remember who I was.

Emilie wanted me there; I had no doubt of that. But she wanted me to be doing something, and the longer I went on not knowing what to do, the more insecure she became.

I wasn't trying to challenge her. But she seemed to take it as a personal attack.

One night she even said it like that. We had finished dinner and I was cleaning up. Emilie was sitting at the kitchen table, under the hanging kitchen light. Her feet were up on the other seat and she was peeling the label off her bottle of beer. She was serious and she was concentrating. I had been trying to talk to her but she was not talking back. She wanted to talk about work again.

'I don't get it,' she said. 'You liked your job, the one in Jaibalito, at the school. You loved that job. Why not do that again?'

'I don't know. I did like it. But things are different now. Things have changed. I want something else to what I wanted then.'

'Like what? What do you want?'

'I don't know. Something else.'

'Oh my god. Come on, Ruth.'

I could feel how frustrating I was for her. I even agreed with her. But I couldn't do anything differently. 'Emilie, I just need time.'

'You've been here two months. How much time do you need? It's like you think you're better than me.'

I stopped washing the dishes and turned around. 'That's not what I think. I don't know how long I need. I'm trying. That's the part you can't see. You have to believe me.' I threw the tea towel on the floor, and then I calmed down and picked it up, but I folded it with intensity.

Emilie took a breath. She put her feet on the floor. She beckoned for me to sit on the chair where she had been resting her feet.

She took my hands in hers. 'You've been through a hard time. I know it is true. It's been a hard time for you.'

I waited to hear what she would say next.

'But you can't live in the hard times forever. It's time to move on. To get on with your life.'

'That is what I am trying to do. Damn it.' I was really frustrated now. I pulled my hands free. She didn't get it, not one little bit. She had no idea. 'That's the whole point. I am trying to get on with my life. Not return to the past. If I went to work in a school, I'd be going back, or trying to hold on to something that I don't have anymore. I'm trying to find something new.'

Emilie breathed out and puffed out her cheeks. She raised her shoulders with academic arrogance. 'Well, I don't get it.'

'No, you don't.'

'That's exactly what I just said.' She walked out of the room.

I knew that Emilie was running out of patience with me, and I even understood why. To anyone, Emilie was the reasonable one. But I couldn't help it. I couldn't do things any other way. I was waiting for the way forwards to appear and I couldn't make it come any more quickly than this.

Usually I went to bed early and Emilie stayed up late. Tonight, I stayed in the living room, on the couch, pretending to read. Instead of reading, I thought about all the things that Emilie had said that night. I thought about how she was probably right about it all, and it made me wonder what I was even doing here. I didn't think I had made a mistake by coming here. Not yet. The mistake was everywhere, the mistake was the whole world, and the mistake was inside me. It didn't matter where I was. The mistake would follow me.

When I thought Emilie would be asleep I went upstairs to go to bed. I brushed my teeth; the bathroom tiles were cold on the soles of my feet. I turned off the light and the sudden darkness was a shock. I stepped through the dark carefully.

Emilie was lying very still in the bed. I couldn't hear her breathing. I lay with the covers half over me. The fan above the bed turned so slowly that I could see each blade separately. I wasn't tired.

In the darkness of the night, Emilie spoke to me. 'Do you ever think about Carmen?' She spoke quietly, as though she was speaking to herself. She sounded like a different person now to the one that she had been downstairs.

I thought about it. 'I think I am thinking about her all the time. Not thinking, really. More feeling her. I feel her almost all the time.'

Emilie made a small understanding sound.

I put my arms under my head. I thought some more. 'It's like she's with me. Or she has become part of me or something. It's hard to explain. I feel like she's here all the time. Sometimes I forget and I go the whole day without remembering her. Then I remember, and there she is, right with me, and she was there all along. She was there even when I didn't notice her.'

Downstairs, the fridge began to hum. Emilie was quiet. I wondered if I had said too much. It was the truth, what I had said. But maybe it had been too much. Sometimes Emilie went hard when I spoke too honestly. But she didn't go hard this time. Maybe it was the night. Maybe it was the dark. Maybe it was because we were not looking at each other but looking at the ceiling and the pattern of the streetlights. Maybe it was to do with Emilie getting thin and drawn and vulnerable.

Then she spoke, and her words sounded like spring. 'It sounds nice. Like an eternal friend.' Emilie was giving me a small gift.

'An eternal friend. Yes, that's it.' Tears came to my eyes and one tear even fell down.

Emilie put her hand on my chest. 'Don't forget, though. You still need to live your own life. You need to go on.' She had become the old Emilie again.

'Go on. What does that mean? I am going on. This is what going on looks like to me.'

We were both quiet again and it was different from the quiet before. Each one was on our own and a little tougher now. Emilie didn't understand. I was sure she was thinking the same about me.

But Emilie had got it – an eternal friend. She had understood at least that part of it. She was quiet but she was not asleep. I rolled over and lay my head on her chest. She pulled me in. We lay in the dark. A third kind of quiet entered between us. This one felt the most real. I felt that we were young and trying to figure things out. We had lived enough by now to be confused about life. We had lived through our twenties and half of our thirties too and neither of us could get it right. I thought maybe we had it wrong. We had thought it was about getting life right. But maybe it was more about putting up with the wrong. Accepting that we would get it wrong no matter how hard we tried.

An eternal friend. Emilie hadn't talked like that before. I wondered what unseen place lay inside her that came up with a comment like that. I felt I didn't know her at all. I had been judging her. I had thought she was small.

We fell asleep without saying goodnight. That night, Emilie and I were our own country. We belonged to the same place and had our own nationality. We had become a family.

24

THAT WEEKEND, EMILIE WENT AWAY on a work trip to the mountains. She left on Friday afternoon. On Friday night I walked through the house in bare feet. I made toast and watched TV. I turned the TV off and listened to the wind. I went to bed early but I couldn't sleep.

I got up and made a cup of tea. I leant against the bench and held the tea close to me; I sipped it slowly and breathed in the steam. I hadn't turned on the kitchen light and moonlight shone on the kitchen floor. I looked out the window and the moonlight was shining on the courtyard ground outside. It was ghostly. A cat jumped on top of the fence and walked from post to post. The cat was much bigger than a normal cat that would be somebody's pet. This cat was wild and muscular. I thought I was invisible, but the cat suddenly turned and looked at me. It stared at me, totally still, for a very long time. I stared back. We were kind of locked in. The cat was so still that the scene outside was like a photograph.

I put the cup in the sink and my movement broke the trance. The cat started moving again, walking along the top of the fence. When it got to the end of the row, it didn't turn back; it jumped down into the courtyard on the neighbour's side.

The next morning, for no reason, I felt happy. I had slept well after the cat, and I had slept in and when I woke, I was feeling refreshed. I made breakfast and I laid it out on the table the way that Emilie had done for me on my first day here. I laid out bread, butter and jam, a plate, a knife and a spoon. Then I sat down and put my feet on the chair and poured coffee and added the milk. I ate and drank slowly. I had time. I put down my book and looked outside and stared. I felt good. I did not know why I felt so good. I felt like a bird about to fly.

I looked over the small pile of books I had put on the living-room shelves. I remembered when I had carved in Jaibalito. It had calmed me down back then. Behind the pile of books was my carving kit. I pulled out the case and I held it and it felt heavy. I searched the house for a piece of wood that I could carve. Any wood would do. I couldn't find anything anywhere. Emilie kept an ordered house and she got rid of everything. I remembered last night, and the cat, and I went into the courtyard. At the back of the courtyard there was a garden shed and the shed had a padlock but the lock wasn't closed. I opened the door. The door was stiff.

Inside it was dark and there was a lot of old stuff that wasn't Emilie's. There were pieces of furniture, an old wooden bed that had been taken apart and was in lots of small pieces. I took all four of the narrow legs and unscrewed the bed posts from the frame.

I laid out newspaper on the living-room floor. I carved all afternoon. The carving was different this time from when I carved in Jaibalito. An energy came from within. The hours flew by and suddenly it was dark and it had gotten cold. I stood up and turned on the living-room light. I got a jumper from the wardrobe upstairs. I turned on the light in the kitchen too. I made toast and tea and ate it quickly. I went back to carving on the living-room floor.

The next day I set up a desk in the corner of the living room. In the shed there was an axe and I took the larger pieces of wood and made smaller pieces to carve figurines. I made a pile and placed them on newspaper, leaning them against the living-room door. I carved for the rest of the day.

Emilie came home on Sunday night and looked into the room with an eyebrow raised. 'You've been carving?'

'Yeah. All weekend.'

'Okay.' She raised her eyebrows and puffed out her cheeks, but she was smiling too. She seemed bemused. She walked to the other room.

That night, we ate smoked trout. Emilie put it on a plate and we peeled off the orange flesh in pieces with our hands. We watched a movie on Emilie's old TV. The picture was not very clear. I put my legs on Emilie and she rested her arms on me. Outside, it was windy, then it started to rain. It smelled like a storm was on the way.

From then on, Emilie was more patient with me. I carved every day but I did other things too. I cleaned and I shopped and I started going out in the community. I visited the school, knowing Emilie would be proud, and I asked if I could volunteer.

They said yes, and I arranged to volunteer for one day a week. I lived harder than I had been living before. When I cleaned the house, I cleaned harder and deeper. I shopped with more intensity. And I carved every afternoon.

In the evenings these days, Emilie spoke to her mother. She went outside to speak to her, and she came back into the living room and she rubbed her face with her hands. She told me about the conversation they had had, and she sat close to me. When I went to bed now, Emilie came to bed too, instead of staying up later like she used to do.

One night she came in from talking outside and she put her head on her knees. She covered her face with her hands for a while and then tried to blow her mood away by shaking her body and her head. She ran both of her hands through her hair. Her face was tight. She seemed as though she was about to cry. She bit her lip.

'Ruth,' she said, and she turned to me. Her face was full of anguish. 'I think I need to go back home.' She breathed out hard. 'She's sounding more and more confused. She has her neighbour and my cousin, but I'm her daughter. I should check on her.' Emilie sighed and ran her hand over her face. She looked out the window into the night. She looked tired and old. She turned back to me. 'You'll be okay?'

'I'll be fine. You should check on her.' Emilie looked at me with a weary smile. She nodded and didn't say anything.

—

That night, I stayed up carving all night. Emilie had gone to bed early and she slept a long time. When she woke, I was still up, high from tiredness. Emilie was happy and that made me relaxed.

It was Saturday. We went out for breakfast and then we went for a walk. We walked all the way to the edge of town, which we never normally did, and right on the very edge of town, where the houses stopped and there was just dry land, there was a house with a large garden and in the garden there was an old man.

The man was gardening and he ignored us both and Emilie looked around. She became excited.

'Ruth, look!' she whispered, and she grabbed my arm. She pointed to different places in the garden, pointing to each area one by one.

I turned to where she was pointing and I saw them, carved statues, made of wood. The statues were creatures that came up to your knees. They were supernatural creatures that seemed as though they were from some kind of mythology.

'Ruth, you have to go and talk to him,' Emilie said quietly.

I didn't know why she was more excited than me. She had never been interested in my carving before. But that was before, and she was changing. I didn't talk to him that day. But on the way back home I mapped out the directions in my mind. Maybe, one day, I would go back.

That evening Emilie booked tickets to go back to Switzerland. She would leave in one week.

25

With Emilie gone, I worked very hard and I didn't leave the house very much. I went straight to carve when I woke up in the mornings, and I worked right through until lunch. I went for a walk and bought tacos at the stand beside the market. Then I slept and when I woke I was ready to go again. Then I repeated the whole cycle again: cup of tea, work, eat. I worked late into the nights.

Emilie called one day. She sounded sad.

'Ruth? It's worse than I thought. I'm going to have to stay another few weeks.'

It was Saturday afternoon. Emilie had been gone for one week. I was attempting to carve a shape, a gnome I had dreamt of that night. I had tried for hours and I couldn't get it right. I threw my knife at the wall and I made a guttural sound. The knife made a dent and landed on the ground and it spun around. I looked at the knife, scared of myself and the crazed person I had become. I picked up the wood and decided that I had better go and see the old man.

On the way to his house, I was nervous and I rehearsed what I would say. The day was hot and dry. A fine dust lifted off the ground and I could taste it in my mouth as I walked. It tasted like chalk. Everything around me was brown, the ground, the buildings, the fences around each area of house and yard. A mangy dog came and followed me. It was sweet, but it smelled, and I felt sorry for it.

The old man was in the garden when I arrived and I stood outside his gate. He saw me looking at his statues. He stood up and wiped the sweat of his face, tilted his hat and he squinted at me. Then he brushed his hands on his pants and he said, 'Are you coming in?'

Up close, the old man was feminine. He was almost like an old woman. He was both. He smelled of wood and oil and grease and he wore overalls and he had coarse hands. He waved his arms around him and he smiled as he showed me his garden. There was a pebble garden to the side and in front were wild tough Mexican bushes and the largest of his statues. There was a winding path that led to the front door; the door was the shape of an arch. The house was painted pale brown and it reminded me of gingerbread.

Inside his house was circular and it smelled warm, of different spices. The tables and couch were covered in cloth. He told me he had built the house himself, by hand, and that it had taken him many years. It still wasn't complete, he said, looking around with tenderness. He waved his arms around again like he had done in the garden; I understood he wanted me to go and explore. He walked to the stove and took out a pot and ran the water. I walked around, feeling shy. One large corner of the living room was devoted to his carving, and there were half-finished works and tools and shavings on the desk and on the floor. I walked to this area and I looked at his tools.

'That is where I work,' the old man said, looking up from the saucepan where he was making coffee. He made a special brew, with cardamom, cloves and cinnamon and I understood why his house smelled like this.

The old man poured me a cup in a handmade coffee mug made of clay. He poured one for himself and then he took me to the corner where he worked. He sat at his stool and started explaining things. I hadn't told him that I carved. But somehow he already knew.

He told me that his name was Hans and he was from Germany. He had lived here for many years. He moved to Mexico when he was thirty-one to follow 'the woman of his dreams'. The woman, he told me, 'blew up in smoke', and he made a noise and a sign with his hands. But he had stayed and he said it was then that his real life finally began.

At first he lived in Morelia. Then he went with some Americans to San Miguel de Allende. 'It was the sixties,' he said. 'We were crazy then. Hippies were everywhere. And they all ended up in

San Cristóbal de las Casas, or San Miguel de Allende. I don't like humidity, so I went to San Miguel. I was a hippy too.'

There had been a trend among the hippies to learn handicrafts. 'At first I learnt weaving with straw, making these types of sandals and things.' One day a Mexican friend was playing around with wood and a knife. 'He was making the most incredible things with that tiny pocketknife. I asked him if he would teach me and he showed me right there, in the middle of the park.' He laughed out loud, healthy and long.

I didn't know why, or what was funny. But I liked to hear him laugh like that and he felt good to be around.

After that, Hans wanted to learn the proper way, the way you learnt a trade in Germany. 'I searched for a school. I looked everywhere. I asked around. The people laughed at me.' They sent him to a different place and each place he arrived, he was told to go to somewhere else.

'Finally, I knew I needed to learn on my own. That no-one could teach me what I needed to know. I found things in books. I practised a lot. I made many mistakes. I carved and I threw them out.'

I laughed inside, remembering my time in Jaibalito when I had thrown my carvings into the lake, and later, when I had burnt them.

Hans kept talking. 'I tried to find books wherever I could and I ordered books from overseas. I learnt about carving from everywhere. I found that every country all around the world has its own different technique. It didn't matter where I was anymore. I was learning from books, and I was practising. I practised all the time. It changed my life. Carving became its own special thing.'

'But how did you end up in Pátzcuaro?'

'Here? Ah.' He smiled, his eyes twinkling, an ancient elf. 'Ah, yes, Ruth. Maybe someday I will tell.'

I spent a lot of time there when Emilie was away. Hans enjoyed his life and he enjoyed being alive. He liked combinations in life.

'Ruth, coffee goes with sun and the outdoors. Tea goes with the kitchen table and a fireplace. Work goes with morning, of course, and any regretting that needs to be done should be done in the early evening, when the gods are close, and can hear.' He pointed a long finger at me. 'There's nothing wrong with regretting, Ruth. Regretting just means you are learning things.'

His house smelled of toast when I arrived. That was another combination that he liked. 'Toast with jam, and always tea. Coffee goes with pastries, toast goes with tea.' He worked and he lived for work and all he cared about was work, but somehow his love for his work spilled out around him and turned his life into a beautiful thing. He told me how he had been lonely all his life and how he always thought that one day he wouldn't be lonely anymore. That somehow life would save him from it.

'But, Ruth.' He leant forward. He almost whispered now. 'It is something wonderous. Like a pearl that is made when the sand gets in. The sand gets in, it shouldn't get in, it is not meant to be there. But it gets in and it rubs and it rubs for many years and then—' he opened his hands out wide '—a beautiful pearl. The priceless thing. The thing that everybody wants.' He became serious. 'But it takes many years, Ruth. It is an art to survive those difficult years. To wait for the beautiful thing.'

He would not teach me but he let me come to his house and watch him work whenever I wanted to. He would not teach me because no-one had taught him and he believed in finding the thing for yourself. I sat near him and I watched him carve. I listened to him and I watched how he lived, just daily things, how he made the coffee. He was how I wanted to be.

26

When Emilie came home she could barely look at me. She was tired and thin and almost grey. Her skin had become papery. I applied to her what I had learnt with Hans about the combinations. Toast with tea. Work with morning. Coffee and sun and bare feet. I made up my own combinations too. Fried capsicums and cheese. Fresh air and mornings. Thick socks and early evenings. Dusk and gentle questioning.

Emilie was too tired to see what was happening, and it didn't matter anyway. I was becoming something I wanted to be, and now I was able to help her. She went back to work but she came home early; she didn't work on the weekends anymore. She wanted to spend weekends with me, at home, or close to it. We went on short walks around the neighbourhood. We walked slowly, not going far. Emilie looked at things but didn't point anymore. But I knew she wasn't withdrawing from me. We had never been closer before.

For the first time since I met Emilie, I felt that she wasn't pretending. I felt as though she was showing what lay beneath her efficient self. I knew there were more layers underneath and that this layer had to be on top; it had to be loosened up and blown away. After that she would get to the layers underneath, but for now she needed to be like this, however dysfunctional it made her. I knew all of this because I had been there before; I had done it too. I had failed and I had fallen apart.

I went to see Hans during the week and I carved at nights and on weekends. Mainly Emilie needed me to be there, just around, nearby, like a mother, or a pet. I could be there carving and I carved all the time, in the living room, leaning against the living-room wall. I carved when Emilie was watching TV and I took breaks to sit and watch shows with her. When we went on walks, I did what Emilie once did; I looked at the world, and I engaged with it. I pointed things out and I got new ideas for things that I could carve. Emilie nodded and looked at the street.

I heard Emilie's phone conversations from the other room. At first she spoke a lot and tried to change her mother's mood. Then I heard her arguing back, defending herself against a silent attack. Now when they spoke, Emilie hardly talked at all; she nodded for an hour or more. When she got off the phone she cried silently. When she came back into the room, her face was cold and wet with tears.

For the first time in her life, Emilie had no plan. She could only wait. She couldn't move; she couldn't change anything.

She couldn't change jobs, or cities. I realised she was waiting for her mother to die.

Two friends she knew from an NGO came by to visit. Emilie had not been to the bar for some time and they had not seen her at the other expat things. I wouldn't have called them friends, but Emilie did. I watched them look at the house and then at Emilie. They were observing carefully. They had brought tamales and a bottle of wine. I set out four plates under the fluorescent light that hung above the kitchen table. Emilie tried. She smiled and talked and asked questions too, but she was grey. The women were polite. When they left there was a distance between them and Emilie. They had tried and they could not cross the gap that had formed between the world and Emilie. They left and Emilie closed the door and went to sit on the couch. She turned on the TV and pulled up a rug and lay down underneath it.

I was not worried. I knew what was happening, and I knew it was good, though it didn't seem like it. I knew it was a process and that it would take time. I knew it was a good thing.

I went to see Hans a few times each week. I walked through the swinging gate and when it creaked and I was walking up the path, Hans opened the door and left it open and he walked back inside; I came in by myself. By the time I entered he was in the kitchen, putting coffee in the pot. He talked to me about what he had been thinking that day, that moment before I came in. Hans bought the newspaper every morning and he cut out articles, which he left in piles on one end of the kitchen table. The table was covered with things like this, things that Hans thought were interesting.

He had one small area at the end where there was space for him to eat.

His desk smelled of sawdust and metal tools. I used to just sit and watch him work but lately I had been bringing in my own pieces and I worked on them next to him. I took a piece from my pocket and unfolded the cloth that I had wrapped it in. This piece that I had been working on scared me a bit. It seemed almost alive. I put the cloth back in my pocket and I started working on it.

After a while, Hans paused and looked over at me and my figurine. He peered and then he took it from me and he held it up to his face. Hans was tiny, with small bones, his tiny denim overalls and drooping, sandy skin. There were deep lines all over his face. He was radiant. His energy stretched out from his body in all directions and some of it reached me. He lifted his finger and pointed at me. 'This is excellent, Ruth,' he said, and he handed the figurine back to me.

While we worked, Hans made up things about each figure that he made. He said things like, 'This one sleeps on the floor in a thatched hut and has no furniture and it doesn't even need to cook its food – it eats its corn raw.' Another time he said, 'This one has long hair as thick as rope and she lives on the other side of a river from a town. When she wants to get across, she swings her long braid over a tree branch and crosses the river like Tarzan. In this way she is able to go to the town whenever she needs, but no-one from the town can come to her.' Sometimes he laughed; sometimes he was serious.

Now, when I was carving at home, before I showed the figurines to Hans, I tried to imagine the details of their lives the way that Hans did with his. I made up my own things. 'This one only eats olives and has a whole pot of them in his hut. When he is hungry, he eats just one olive and that gives him so much energy that he can fly around the town, looking at things from the sky. The olives are so precious that he guards them closely, and when he is not flying, he is like a rabid dog. Nobody in the town comes to visit him but they love to watch him fly.'

I told these stories to Emilie while I was working on them at night. At first she laughed, weary and polite, the way a sick person laughs when they don't have the energy to find things funny anymore. Then she started asking me. She leant over from where she was lying on the couch and she asked, 'What does this one do?' And I told her and she laughed, properly now, quietly, but true.

One day I brought my newest figurines to Hans. He put on his glasses and examined them carefully. He frowned. He took his glasses off and turned to me. 'Tell me, what do these ones do?'

One afternoon I was preparing a fresh set of carvings to show Hans. I had started making labels to go with each one and on each label I drew pictures too. I took these to Hans and he read the labels seriously and I felt that he really cared about them, as though the figurines were real people. He read the labels and then he inspected the carvings. He never gave me any advice on them, but I could tell from where he touched each one and from the specific sounds he made how I could improve them.

I had twelve new carvings and I sat at the kitchen table finishing labels with the stories of their lives. When I was done, I placed each one carefully in the box that I carried them in. There were three carvings left and I didn't want to put them in the box; I wanted to send them to the boys.

I had not heard anything about the boys since I was fired. I had not heard about them when I was in Panajachel or when I was in Jaibalito. I calculated how old they would be and I tried to imagine their lives. I couldn't imagine anything.

The three figurines I had left were my favourites. One was a monster with angel wings, and he was strong, but kind, and he could fly. The villagers thought that he was scary and they left him alone but when one of them had a special wish he flew to them and he granted it. This one I chose for Eduardo. One was green and had a round tummy and carried a pot of honey wherever he went. If he didn't like something he tipped honey all over it and whatever it was could not move again until it started to rain. If he liked something he gave it a spoon from a pile that he carried around as well, and he invited it to share in his pot and have a spoonful whenever it liked. This one I chose for Rafael. For Josue I chose one who had surfboards as feet and could cross any water that he came across. That meant that he could live anywhere and not worry about people or roads. He was free.

I packed them up into a smaller box and I sent them off with a note. I didn't know if they were still living there, in the house in Panajachel, or if the mother would even pass them on to the boys. But I didn't care. I had made something for them.

I took the box to the post office and sent it off. I felt both happy and sad now, and I didn't know where to go or what to do. It was Friday afternoon. I had finished early today. I could go to the expat bar; everyone would be there by now, or they would be there soon. But I didn't want to go there. I wanted to climb a hill, or walk to water, the way that I did at the lake.

I just went home instead. I started making dinner. Emilie would be home soon. I went upstairs and opened the window and I tidied up the bedroom. I lay on the bed. I felt heavy and then I cried. But then the crying was all done and I went downstairs, still sad, but now light.

Emilie came home tired that day. We ate outside in the courtyard that night, under the open sky. Emilie put her feet on my lap. We didn't talk much. Emilie picked food off the plate with her hands. It took a long time to get dark that night. Summer must be coming. A bird called through the sky.

27

Emilie's mother died in the night. It was morning before the nursing home called, which was evening by then in Mexico. Emilie was not surprised. For weeks before her mother died, she had given up the fight. I saw now she had been fighting against the circumstances of her life. I saw it only now that she had given up. She seemed like a new person, sad, but complete. She was defeated in a way she never thought she would be. I had failed and I had expected it. Emilie had always thought she would succeed.

Those last few weeks had been so painful and tight that when Emilie's mother finally died, it was a relief. The house could breathe. Emilie had been working at the office late on the day that she found out. When she came home, she didn't come all the way in, but stood in the doorway and announced, 'She's dead,' as though to a crowded room.

That night Emilie didn't eat anything but sat at the table out of habit while I ate. She seemed so small. But she was light now.

She was sad, but she glowed. In the morning, Emilie was downstairs, sitting at the kitchen table, drinking tea and scrolling on her phone. She looked at me and she smiled and I could see that she was soft and tired now. The night had been good for her.

'The funeral is in one week. I've checked the flights; there's one in three days. I didn't know … Well, I was wondering … I mean, I wasn't sure …' She trailed off.

I leant down and held her head close to me. I put my face next to hers. 'Book a ticket for me too. I want to come.' She smelled of sleep and sweat and grief. I pressed my face to her face and I could feel her salty tears.

We arrived in Bern at three in the afternoon. I had to remind myself that this was not a holiday. I was not here to have a good time. It was beautiful, though. Clear and old. We went straight to the house we had rented to stay in for the week. Emilie did not want to stay at her mother's and she didn't want to stay with family. From the airport to the house, which was in the centre of town, I looked around. I loved the brown buildings and the steep roofs. I loved the tiny flower boxes and the railings on the old houses. But I was not here on holiday.

The funeral was to be held three days after we arrived. Emilie was busy with preparations. There were other family members involved but in the end they all went to Emilie to make the final decisions.

Emilie didn't cry at the funeral. I was waiting for her to cry. She didn't cry at the reception either. Old, pale, Swiss relatives came to her with both hands. She received them but she didn't say much.

She didn't say much when we got back to the house. She sat in a chair by the window and looked out on the street. It had been raining. The streets were wet. She sat there with a cup of tea, which she didn't touch for an hour or more while I busied myself. I made fresh tea and replaced her cold cup with a hot cup on the table.

She grabbed my arm and looked up at me. 'I'm the only one left,' she said.

I didn't know when she decided it, but she told me in the taxi on the way to the airport to catch our flight. I had been expecting it, though.

'Ruth, I think I need to move back home.'

'Home. You mean Switzerland?'

'Yes. Here. Home.' She paused. 'Would you think about coming with me?'

I could hear the heater fan from the front of the car. The car smelled new and it was very smooth. I didn't have to think and I spoke with my whole body. 'I'll come with you. We're family.'

Outside the night was dark and the roads were wet. City lights sparkled in the rain. The tyres of the passing cars splashed water. We paused at a red traffic light. The engine stopped. There was no sound now. The light went green. The car moved forwards.

It didn't take long for things to fall into place when we got back home to Mexico. Emilie gave notice to her job when she returned. She talked to her boss and told her what was happening. She would still be able to work on projects with the university, her boss had said to her. They would stay in touch, they would figure something out, the boss said. Emilie thanked her. But she didn't really care.

For the next few weeks we lived in limbo; not in Pátzcuaro anymore but not anywhere else yet. Emilie went to work and I visited Hans and I carved a little. But during the day I packed, or I cleared things out or I did practical things like arranging to get the electricity turned off.

At nights now, instead of watching TV, Emilie went through her things and decided what she wanted to keep. She packed up boxes and sent them to Europe by ship. The neighbour next door had started learning guitar. He was practising Bach. He played the same notes over and over and then he started again from the start. During the time that we were packing and getting ready to leave, he improved, but it was slow.

With two weeks to go, we were organised. We had sent by ship everything we wanted to keep that we could not carry with us. Things were ready and our lives felt neat. Leaving felt almost right.

But I had a feeling that wouldn't go away. It was to do with Carmen, and the lake. Since my life had gotten better here, I had not been thinking about her, or it. I had separated what had happened over there into a different container in my life. I didn't want to say goodbye to Carmen. I had been putting it off. I wanted her to live on forever inside me and I thought that if I visited her grave, she would die.

But she was already dead. I didn't know what I was trying to do. Carmen had already died and there was nothing I could do that would make her die again, or keep her alive anymore. Carmen could not die twice.

28

I WENT BACK TO THE lake the quick way, by plane. I flew there and arranged to come back by bus. I didn't like flying but I wanted to get there quickly, before I changed my mind. I arranged with Dwain to stay at his house; he wouldn't be there, and I was relieved.

The plane landed in Guatemala City and from there I caught the bus to the lake. I watched the narrow winding roads, I smelled the mountain air, I looked at the huts, which were just like the hut that I lived in, in Jaibalito.

At Dwain's, I put my bag on the floor. I would sleep on the couch that night. I did not want to sleep in the room that I had thought of as mine when Carmen was alive.

Then I went out to walk around. It was sad being back here, after being away. I loved it here but I couldn't let myself love it now that I was leaving and wouldn't see it again. I didn't listen to the gentle sound of the waves as they fell on the shore.

When the afternoon sun hit the lake from the side and set the water sparkling, I didn't look; I let my eyes pass over it. I didn't listen to the neighbourhood chickens cluck and scratch in the dirt, nor did I feel the crunch of the path under my feet. I didn't smell the trees or the dirt or listen to the wind. I loved this place and I was leaving it. And I was leaving Carmen too.

In the morning I woke early to a lot of light. Dwain's house had windows everywhere. I got up straight away and I packed my small backpack with a bottle of water, and some food. The day was dry and already warm. I put on my hat and I borrowed a bandana of Dwain's to wet and tie around my neck. On my way out, I clicked the gate closed and I walked in the direction of Miguel's house.

Before I got there, I met Miguel, coming from the other way. He didn't seem surprised to see me. We said hello and he didn't ask me anything and I didn't explain. I just asked him about the way to Carmen's grave. He turned around and pointed to the white cross on the hill, and he gave me the directions. You had to follow the path halfway to San Marcos and from there, there was a path leading straight up. It would take about an hour to walk there, he said. It wasn't far, he said, but it was steep. You had to step carefully.

On the way up, the sun was at my back. I could feel the lake stretch out behind me but I did not stop to look at it. I walked without stopping, at a steady pace. I found the turn-off that Miguel had told me about. I took it and suddenly the path was steep. Yellow rocks slipped and fell around me with each step. The path narrowed and pointy shrubs scratched my arms and legs. I was sweating so much that sweat ran into my eyes, and it stung and made my eyes water. I didn't stop. I got to the top and I looked around for the next path that Miguel had told me to take. It should be to my right, and I looked around and I searched in between the shrubs. Miguel had said it was an overgrown path. Nobody came up here to visit anymore, he had said. This was the cemetery for foreigners; the local people must do something else with their dead.

I finally found a patch of flattened grass and I followed it and it became a path. I followed the path through the thick shrubs and then it opened out into a clearing. Now I was on the very top of the hill. The clearing was surrounded by trees on all sides except on the side that faced the lake. The cemetery was tiny.

I stood for a moment and took it all in. I had thought it would be windy up here, but it was as still as a summer's day. I tried to imagine how Carmen would like it, being buried all the way up here. I felt her roll her eyes at me and say, 'Ruth, I'm not actually *in* the grave. I've gone away; the grave is for the rest of you, to feel like you have somewhere to go when you miss me. I don't care, I'm gone, I'm not even listening to you.' Even from within my own mind, Carmen could make me feel small. But I laughed as well. I got her point. This was fine. I didn't have to be so dramatic.

The white cross was in the middle of the clearing and the graves were scattered all around. I read their names: all foreigners. Yes. The locals must go somewhere else. Carmen's grave was off to the side, almost as if she had designed it like that, to show her disdain for this formality. It was peaceful, though. More peaceful than I had expected it to be. I could imagine sleeping here. I would sleep well here, I thought, next to Carmen's grave.

I stood in front of her grave but then I felt dramatic again, like I was in an American movie. So I sat next to her grave just like I sat next to her when she was alive. For a long time I didn't say anything. I sat, and I felt her, and I watched the lake. I tried to understand what it was that I felt. I tried to separate what I felt for Carmen and the lake and I found that I could not; inside me, they were the same. I picked up a stick and I drew in the dirt and I used the stick to hit my feet. The sun was high and it was hot and it was burning me. I heard a noise and I looked behind; there was no-one there. I threw the stick on the ground, suddenly strong and covered in rage.

'Fuck you, Carmen. Fuck. You. Go to hell.' It felt good to say all of this. It was not what I had expected to say. 'Fuck you for judging me, even from the grave. Do you know how much easier it is to be dead than alive? So fuck you. I am doing my best. You didn't even try.' A tear rolled down the side of my cheek, and dried.

But she had tried. I was quieter now. She had tried and what she had tried had not worked. She had tried in every way she knew and she had died because she had tried everything. Her ways had not worked. That was not her fault.

It was not her fault that she was dead and it was not my fault that I was alive. It felt like we had each been assigned to two different groups on a school camp. I imagined her in the afterlife, making friends and doing things that I couldn't join in with.

And I imagined my life, my life now and my future. I had moved to Pátzcuaro and soon I would be living in Switzerland. Carmen had never been there before. She had not been to Pátzcuaro either. I imagined myself making new friends that Carmen wouldn't meet. I would live in houses that she wouldn't see. And I would grow older and then I'd be old and Carmen would be young and a memory.

I had come here for something other than this. I had thought I had come here to say goodbye to Carmen. But Carmen was saying goodbye to me.

Dwain was mainly staying in Panajachel, sleeping on couches of friends. After Jaibalito I arranged to meet up with him. I stayed in a hotel and met him in a café. I thought he would stay at Carmen's house but when I said that he looked at me as though it was cursed.

Dwain didn't look well and he didn't look well in a way that seemed permanent. He wore the same clothes as before and they were older and more worn now; he had put on weight and it made him seem old. He had lost his gentleness and I talked to him but I couldn't see where he was. I searched his face, in his eyes; I listened to the things that he said. The Dwain that I knew was gone. I didn't talk about Carmen or tell him about my visit to her grave.

When Dwain and I said goodbye, I knew I had lost another friend, but this way of losing was slower and more confusing. I missed Dwain how I remembered him, open like the sky, taking us in and trying to say the thing that would help us keep going in our lives. I saw it now; Dwain had not survived.

He had not survived Carmen's death. It had been too much for him. The shock had sent him somewhere else; or else, with Carmen gone, he didn't know how to live. He was biding his time. I thought of the Townes Van Zandt song 'Waiting Around to Die'. Dwain was always out with his friends, and in the days after we met, when I was still in Panajachel, I saw him out the front of the bars. The first time, I stopped to talk to him; he seemed embarrassed and his friends looked on in a mocking way. The next time I saw him, I didn't stop; when he saw me, he turned away.

I left on the bus the next day. The leaving was final this time. It was the end of everything, of Carmen, of Dwain, of the lake. It had all really ended a long time ago, but I had to come back to realise it. Panajachel was over now. I was visiting a different place.

29

On the bus from Guatemala to Mexico, I remembered her. I had not let myself remember her yet. She was so much like a dream that I sometimes thought that I had invented her. I felt like I had two separate lives – the life that had Carmen in it, and the life where she had not existed at all. But on the bus from Guatemala to Mexico, I remembered her, and I saw that she was real. That she had been real all this time. She had existed and she had been my friend. I had loved her. She was real.

The memory was mundane and I was proud of her for coming to me in a mundane way. Maybe she was maturing, in the afterlife. She didn't have to be flamboyant anymore.

I remembered her in the market. When Carmen moved through the market, she almost flounced and her hair shone in the darkness. She walked as though she had been born there, which she had, but she didn't look like it and so it didn't seem right. Even though everyone knew her, people stared. Once, a local told me that the boys in the town were in love with her. Carmen couldn't care less. And she didn't seem interested in relationships. I never even found out if she liked men or women. She seemed beyond all of that. Sort of already complete. I couldn't imagine her in a relationship.

She took me to the market now, and we walked around. She tried on a bracelet made of beads and she didn't want to take it off, so she bought it and left it on. Then we sat down at the counter of a stall and she held her wrist up to the light; she asked me what I thought of it. When I said I liked it she put her arm around me hard and pressed her head into my shoulder.

When we had gone to the market while she was alive, she always bought something. Sometimes it was something simple, like a brown paper bag of nuts or a tamal to eat later at home. Sometimes it was something more elaborate. This time she bought a statue of the Buddha with places in his hands to burn incense sticks. She bought some incense too, not the Guatemalan kind but the type imported from India. It was expensive, but she told me it was worth it.

'It might help me,' she said, and then she laughed. 'I might even learn how to meditate.' She held the statue like a teddy bear. 'I'll put it in the garden,' she said, happily, with hope.

It was more than a memory, and it was too real to be a fantasy. It was a vision. I could feel it was a parallel world and I knew without a doubt that Carmen lived in that world and that she was showing it to me. I didn't know how long the vision lasted. The night beyond the steady coach was black and featureless; the long hours had no markers. I sat with her, bright and warm and clear, and then she faded away.

For the rest of the trip, I tried to return to her; at first I could, and then I could not. The door had closed and now it was a memory and not a vision anymore. I was separate from it. I had felt her, though. I had smelled her hair.

Dawn was grey and very still as we entered the outskirts of Mexico City. People were rising and preparing for work. The bus smelled of other people's sleep and petrol and old food.

It was still early and grey when I waited at the depot for the bus to Pátzcuaro. I bought a coffee in a paper cup. It was weak but very hot. Emilie messaged, 'Did you arrive okay?' I replied, 'In DF. Waiting for the next bus. Home soon.'

Emilie replied with a house and a rose. She had started experimenting with emojis. They often did not make sense.

Emilie met me at the bus when I got back. She looked at me all over like she was looking for something specific which she did not find. We walked to the house and she told me the news from the past few days from her work and the town.

I got back feeling clear. I was ready to leave. I had nothing left here anymore. Emilie had seemed nervous before I went to the lake. She had made a joke, 'Make sure you come back,' which I had thought was strange. Now I understood. But things had changed for me. I had left the lake. I no longer wanted to live there.

The last few days went by quickly. Neither Emilie nor I were sad. When I left the lake to move to Pátzcuaro, I had recounted every last thing: 'the last time I'll make coffee at this stove', 'the last time I'll catch the boat'. I didn't do that here. We had things to do. We had somewhere else that we needed to be.

On the last night all our things were gone and all we had left were two bags. Emilie had cut her hair very short and she wore a dark-green shirt. We ordered a pizza and opened a bottle of wine. I filled two paper cups. I held one up.

'To what?' I said.

'To life?'

'Nah, something else. Life is not one of my favourite things.'

Emilie laughed at me. 'You're so weird,' she said. 'Life is everything. Okay. How about – to Switzerland?'

'For what?'

'I don't know. For accepting us back.'

'It's a place, it isn't a person.' It was weird. I sounded like Carmen, and Emilie sounded like me. 'I know!' I had thought of something. 'To the fight.'

'What the hell are you talking about? What fight? You think you're Mohammed Ali?' Emilie laughed.

I frowned. I thought it had sounded good.

'To the next chapter?' she said.

'Whatever. If you want it to be a corny Hollywood movie.'

'So you do better.'

'I can't.'

'See.'

'How about, goodbye?'

'Yes. Goodbye and fuck off.'

'That's not what I meant.'

Emilie was in hysterics now and because she was laughing, I laughed too. I had thought we were both so poetic and smart, but we couldn't even come up with a decent toast at a dramatic time like this.

We gave up on the toast and just drank our wine and the wine tasted good and the pizza did too. The dark tiles we sat on were cold and hard and we both got stiff. Outside, it was still light.

'One last evening walk?'

'Nah,' Emilie said. 'We've seen it all.'

We went to bed and Emilie was teaching me not to always look behind but instead to look ahead.

As the plane took off I saw Mexico from above and it became distant and small. Emilie leant over me to look out the window. I saw how thin and how sad she was. Skin crinkled around her neck. I suddenly saw how much she had changed. I remembered her on that day we first met. She had been strong; she was alien. I had been small and unsure. How much we both had changed. I rested my head against the seat. I breathed. And it wasn't even over yet.

Acknowledgements

THANK YOU TO MY PARENTS, John and Jeanette Morton, for all your support over the years. Thank you to Alex Dazey and Anna Kelsey-Sugg for your considered and thoughtful feedback on the early manuscript. Thank you to Holly Anderson for allowing us to use your mesmerising artwork on the cover.

Thank you to all of the team at UQP for your culture of care, respect and positivity, which made the preparation of the manuscript for publication a meaningful experience in its own right. Thank you especially to my editor, Lauren Mitchell, for your sensitive reading and nuanced suggestions.

Lastly, a special thank you to my publisher, Aviva Tuffield, for your belief in my work from the beginning, without which this book would not exist.

Winner of the UQP Quentin Bryce Award 2025
The Sun Was Electric Light
Rachel Morton

About the UQP Quentin Bryce Award

The Honourable Dame Quentin Bryce AD CVO is an alumna of The University of Queensland, where she completed a Bachelor of Arts and a Bachelor of Laws before becoming one of the first women admitted to the Queensland Bar. In 1968 Quentin Bryce became the first woman appointed as a faculty member of The University of Queensland's Law School. From 2003 to 2008 she served as the twenty-fourth Governor of Queensland, and from 2008 to 2014 she was the twenty-fifth Governor General of Australia, the first woman to hold the office.

In addition to her professional roles, Quentin Bryce has always been a strong supporter of the arts and Australia's cultural life and is an ambassador for many related organisations, including the Stella Prize and the Indigenous Literacy Foundation. Across many decades she has championed The University of Queensland Press (UQP), its books and authors.

To honour and celebrate her impressive career and legacy, The University of Queensland and UQP have jointly established the UQP Quentin Bryce Award. The award recognises one book on UQP's list each year that celebrates women's lives and/or promotes gender equality.

The inaugural recipient of the award in 2020 was Ellen van Neerven's poetry collection *Throat*, which went on to be recognised in multiple prizes, including winning Book of the Year at the 2021 NSW Premier's Literary Awards. In 2021 the award went to Sarah Walker's exceptional collection of essays,

The First Time I Thought I Was Dying, with its examination of our unruly bodies and minds, and the limitations of consent, intimacy and control. In 2022 the recipient was Mirandi Riwoe's dazzling story collection, *The Burnished Sun*, with its focus on women, especially those who are marginalised and disenfranchised, while in 2023 it was Angela O'Keeffe's *The Sitter*, which reimagines the life of Hortense Cezanne while intricately examining the tension between artist and subject, and between the stories told about us and the stories we choose to tell. Jazz Money's much-anticipated poetry collection *mark the dawn* won the award in 2024. The recipient of the UQP Quentin Bryce Award 2025 is *The Sun Was Electric Light* by debut author Rachel Morton.

'What a special book this is. Tender, poignant and filled with longing for those people and places we've lost – and perhaps never truly found in the first place. Rachel Morton's novel leads us through the ache of grief, for self and others, towards acceptance.' – Dame Quentin Bryce